Substance Abuse

Dennis Foy

Red Hat Books

Substance Abuse

This novel is a work of fiction and the characters and events in it exist only in its pages and in the fevered imagination of the author.

To learn more about the author, log onto www.dennisfoy.org
Go on, do it now, before you get engrossed...

ISBN 0-9543340-2-7

First published in Great Britain 2007 by Red Hat Books,
an Art Impact! imprint
Printed on demand by Lulu.com

Published by
Red Hat Books
an Art Impact! company
Manchester
www.redhatbooks.co.uk

For Pat,
who provides the substance
– but no abuse –
in my life

Prelude

"Murder, then. By Persons Unknown."

"Well it wouldn't be bleedin' suicide, would it? Not with his head and hands cut off..."

"Allright Mark, I get your drift..."

Standing here outside the Coroner's Court in Chelmsford, alongside Sutherland. I loosen my tie and light a cigarette.

I sense him watching as I flip the lid of my Zippo closed. "Speaking of early death..."

"It's probably still less risky than what he was up to."

We say goodbye, he gets into his Omega and I walk over to the Alfa, switching my mobile back on as I go. It rings almost immediately with a message. "Mark. Barrington. Presume we can now get this thing to bed. Verdict as expected? Let me know. Cheers, old love."

This all seems an age on from where it started, in the middle of last summer...

1

Into the Borders, 1998

'*He's put some weight on since he retired.*' I was looking across the swathe of bad-taste carpet towards Eric Cantona. Or maybe it wasn't really Eric the Gaul, just another sad bastard wannabe.

The couple had shuffled into the Truck Drivers' Rest Area – three Formica-topped tables with vinyl-covered chairs and cheap glass ashtrays near the toilet door – just as I was stirring my tea. They switched on the television set mounted high on the wall. She was wearing a livid purple and acid green shell suit that clashed awesomely with the Stewart tartan carpeting. He had on a pair of go-to-hell-print jogging pants, mainly lurid yellow and electric blue camouflage splashes on a grey background. The sort of colours that'd let him hide his legs in Ikea's interior furnishings department. And a red United football shirt. As he turned back from tuning the set to his chosen American comic-soap, I saw the name *Cantona* printed in arched white letters above the number seven on his back. If either had spoken whilst they sat gazing up the screen I might have been able to confirm my suspicions that he was an impostor but they didn't. They sat in silence, oblivious to each other.

My stop had not done anything to help me get my head around the story. None of it made sense, but when you're in my position – a freelance hack with no regular income – you can't afford to miss out on any chance to ease the overdraft. The rumours, according to Mike, had begun doing the rounds of the pit lane a couple of weeks earlier, at a practice session.

"I don't want to tell you over the phone. Can't you get up to Knockhill?"

"Do I have to? I was going to bunk off. Got a lot to do–"

"It'll be worth it, honest. You could make a fortune out of the story..."

"Mike, I've just got back from Le Mans, and I'm knackered. I wasn't planning on doing the Scottish round. Can't you just tell me what it's all about?"

"No. You never know who's listening. I have to see you. You'll have to come up here. It's so big it'll really be worth your while."

"Can't we just meet up next week, once you're back home?"

"it won't keep that long. I have a feeling something's going to happen up here..."

By the time he rang off I was assured that there was something to it. Someone, in one of the teams, had started using the cover of the series as a smuggling operation. And nobody was saying any more than that.

I stubbed out what was probably my fifteenth Benson & Hedges of the day. Drained the last of the pale and uninteresting liquid passed off as tea, left the doughnut that I had abandoned after two bites, and picked up my phone. Mr & Mrs Cantona were still gazing, rapt and expressionless, at the screen when I gave them one last glance and headed out to the car.

So how to get to the bottom of what Mike told me? All I knew for sure was that I couldn't just barge in and start asking questions; I'd get stonewalled.

As I pulled back onto the A73, I pointed the nose of my much-abused 620 in the general direction of Edinburgh. As the wipers cleared their screen I wished that the forthcoming round of this particular racing series was at Donington or Silverstone, and not up in bloody Scotland.

I have no problem with driving into France, Germany or wherever, but trudging up the M6 and beyond isn't my idea of fun. Especially When it is raining, which it always seems to be when I get north of Lancashire. So when Mike had rung I'd expressed my usual antipathy to driving all the way from Oxfordshire to some god-forsaken place seven hours North. But he'd insisted – and with no other story to occupy my time I decided that I hadn't much choice. I'd have to brave the worst that Scotland could throw at me and go.

The big bloke on the gate glanced at the half-dozen permanent passes on the screen base of my car, and picked out the one that proved I was in possession of media accreditation for this particular series. Not a difficult pass to find, as it was printed on Day-Glo yellow vinyl that was a perfect match for his waterproof coat. He waved me in.

"Straight through the gates over there, and follow the signs for the Competitors Car Park."

Any of the dozens of local farmers would identify the car park as a waterlogged field. I parked up and cursed the weather that had turned a verdant meadow into sticky mud. Pulled my knackered Barbour jacket off the back seat and dragged it on, putting the hood up, and trudged over the brow. Realised that I'd have to wash the mud off my Timberland boat shoes later. I went on through the middle of the pack of motor homes, towards the circuit office.

"Yes, can I help?" smiled the woman behind the high green-painted counter.

"Hi, I'm Mark McDermott, can I sign on please?"

I handed her a credit-card sized plastic tag attached to a bright yellow cord. It was proof of who I was, and that the series organisers considered me sufficiently well-connected to accredit me to the series. It was one of a half-dozen that saved me an awful lot of hassle arranging passes at individual tracks through the course of a racing year. She took it, noted its number on a sheet of paper, got me to sign alongside the entry, and handed the pass back with a smile.

"If you'd like a coffee, there's a machine just through there." she pointed to a doorway at the far end of the narrow corridor that I was stood in. I thanked her, but declined; when I wandered across the paddock I'd be able to get a good, fresh, filter coffee from the GTD team. Coffee far better than anything that would come out of a vending machine.

All of the big motor racing events – which means this Sports Car series, the Touring Cars and Formula One – are known within the industry as the circus. Dozens of articulated trucks thunder along the road, forty-four tonne behemoths as big as the law allows. Travelling to and from the racetracks in an unstructured semi-official convoy, together but separate, just like touring three-ring circuses.

No matter how foul the weather, no matter how much mud and spray they have acquired on the way, these rolling billboards are washed and polished as soon as they park up. Their colour schemes are mirrored by the racing cars they carry, representing the brands of those companies who pay for everything. And sponsors get pissed off if they can't see their logos.

Then come more livery-matched vehicles. Support vans that carry spares and which double as mobile workshops, with substantial tent awnings that fix to their sides. And last comes the caravan of motorhomes. These become the epicentre of each team, serving as office, as driver briefing centre, as restaurant, as health centre, and as the conference centre where team management and sponsors can meet to thrash out any problems or to congratulate each other on their joint successes.

Once you start to look closely, you realise that for every circus act there is an equivalent character in the personalities of the racing drivers. I sipped my coffee and started to picture each of the main players in this series, to pair them up with circus performers. Will Fellows, a stocky, powerful, ebullient character, chasing the championship title with a vengeance and forcing his way to the front, is the strongman act. Then there is Paul Williams, the illusionist – he has the ability to appear through the pack as if from nowhere and steal wins almost by sleight of hand. He hates the limelight, but loves the power that his style brings with it. A tightrope walker? That would have to be Vivien Reid; always so close to the edge, not just because he makes his car dance through the curves of any circuit but also by the way that he is prepared to take risks in aiming for gaps that didn't exist. The clown troupe has to be the pair of Premier-Porsche drivers, David Walls and Michael Rafferty. They make a wonderfully comic double act on the podium and at press calls, but like true clowns mask their consummate skills behind a façade of buffoonery.

I was pondering who would make the best lion tamer – the driver who conquers an unwieldy car and makes it take his commands – when I was snapped out of my reverie by a quiet hello from just behind my left shoulder. It was Mike, the mechanic. Or more accurately race engineer. This is a business where correct titles are very important, regardless of how pretentious they might be. Mike whose telephone call had persuaded me to venture north of the Forth.

"So you came, then."

"Looks like it..."

"Where are you staying? I need to talk to you and this isn't the place. Anyway, I've only got two minutes."

"I haven't booked in anywhere yet. Any ideas?"

"We're in a little hotel about five miles up the road, the Inverloch. Why don't you see if you can get in there? That way I could come to your room later on and tell you everything without anybody realising that I'm out."

"Have you got their number?"

"Yeah, it's on here."

He handed me the little card that bore his own room details. I took the number down straight into the keypad of my mobile 'phone, and Mike disappeared as I pressed the send button. Two minutes later I had found myself a room for the next couple of nights. This would be expensive – especially as I had no idea what the story was, let alone got anybody to sell it to – but what the hell. I'd been telling myself for years that I ought to spend some time at the friendly Knockhill circuit.

Walking across to the paddock, I heard, then saw, a lone piper. Is the employment situation so bad in Scotland that they've had to make up a job creation scheme? "Got a job for you, Jimmie. D'y'ken how to play 'Banks of the Bonnie Brae' over and over again...?"

Annie came over to me, offered me another coffee – which I of course accepted – and asked if I'd care to stay for lunch. The upside to spending as much time at racetracks as I do is the way that you soon get to know the right people; although there was a sign that read GTD Motorsport: Invited Guests Only a couple of feet away from where I was sat and I wasn't officially invited, I was almost part of the furniture. I'd eaten at this particular team's expense more than a dozen times in the past couple of seasons, and there were three or four other outfits on this same patch of concrete alongside a little grassy knoll that also extended their hospitality to me on a regular basis. It was, so far as I was concerned, a perk of the job and a small price for them all to pay for the generally complimentary things that I'd written about them over the years.

I said yes, thanks, I'd love to have lunch, and flicked open the address book in my Filofax. If I've just committed myself to a hotel bill of two hundred quid, I'd better see if I can sell something to somebody. The first two editors that I rang exchanged pleasantries but told me that they'd already put people onto the meeting, but at the third call I managed to pick something up.

"Hi David, it's Mark. I'm at Knockhill. Anything I can do for you while I'm here?"

"Perfect timing, mate. Can you do me a thousand plus a couple of new pics on Will Fellows? Find out if he's on form. He's on for the title, see what you think."

"No problem. When for?"

"On my desk for Tuesday morning?"

Will Fellows. Numero Uno driver for the team which was at that moment restoring my caffeine levels. The perfect excuse, not that I need one, for sitting at the front of their hospitality unit. Depending on his schedule I could talk to Fellows later today here, or tonight at the hotel. Suddenly Scotland didn't look quite so bleak – things never do when there's a cheque at the end of the rainbow. A two page feature; should more than cover the hotel bill.

As the rain had stopped and I was getting in the way of Annie as she was trying to set the tables for lunch, I figured that it was time to wander over to the side of the track and watch some cars; that, after all, was the official reason that I was there. I prefer to be at tracks for practice sessions than the races themselves; there's a better sensation of what is actually going on. Especially when I can amble gently and unhindered from one pit area to the next and get a real feel for how the machinery is behaving. And the problems that it is bringing with it. Best of all, to get from one part of the track to another is hassle-free as there are no clusters of spectators to get through.

I watched the last half hour of the practice session, studying the cars as they put in laps of the narrow, undulating circuit. From my vantage point on the hillside I watched each car, making mental notes of which cars looked strong and tidy and which obviously still needed some work, and strolled back to the motorhome and a decent lunch.

I had just taken my first forkful of the buffalo mozzarella, tomato and black olive starter course, served with a solitary glass of decently buttery Chardonnay, when I was joined by Ray. Ray Otley, head of the team who were saving me the bother of queuing to buy a burger and chips elsewhere in the circuit.

"Hi Mark, didn't think you'd bother with this one. What brings you up here?"

"Thought I'd better make the effort, y'know, show my readers that I don't just hit the fleshpots of Europe. And I've been asked to do a piece on Will. How's his schedule for today? Is he staying at the Inverloch? And how's it going anyway?"

The conversation was light and friendly, as it always is when Ray is involved. I've known the quiet, gentle and urbane (all three being qualities rare in the paddocks of top-flight motor sport) fifty-something man for more than two decades. We met back in the days when he was a struggling constructor and I was a cub reporter on a local paper in my native Dorset. Over the years we've become firm friends. He called over his press officer, an affable but slightly vague girl called Samantha.

"Can you get Will to clear an hour..." he paused to look at me for confirmation that an hour would be sufficient time "... for Mark this evening?"

She nodded, then looked at me. "Should be no problem. What time would suit you. Mark?"

"Six? Is there a lounge at the hotel I could use?"

"Should be fine. If there are any problems I'll let you know within the next few minutes."

Then Ray filled me in on the good progress that the team was continuing to make. There were occasional interruptions, of course – it's a fact of life in this game that people always need to ask the boss questions during the course of any meal in the motorhome – but as things were going well lunch was as relaxed as it is possible to be.

I watched another hour of practice, had brief chats with people that I knew from some of the other teams, and decided that as it was starting to rain again I might as well head off and check into my hotel. With a bit of luck I could get a quiet hour to myself. And I'd still have time to put together my question sheet for the driver that I would be meeting later.

There was a quiet tap on my door at a little before eleven. I was gazing at the television, watching an advertisement for sanitary towels and wondering. Could there be an entire generation of young girls who have emotional crises when they realise that they don't have blue emissions like those they use to show how absorbent the towels are? I pulled myself off the bed and answered the door; it was Mike.

"So what's it all about, then?" I asked him, as I stretched back out on the bed and he perched himself onto the edge of the compact armchair that occupied one corner of the room.

"It's all rumour, mate, but the word is that Tel Martin's team have just lost their sponsorship deal, and they're going to replace it with coke. Not the drink, the drug. From what I've been told Martin's supposed to be into bringing drugs into the country big-style."

"So why tell me? Why not take it to plod?"

"You're a journalist, aren't you? You should be able to investigate it. I got done about four years ago for possession, nothing much, just a bit of smoke, but all the same the last thing I want is hassle from the old bill."

The pulsing vein on Mike's temple was a dead give-away to the fact that he was wound up, a fact underlined by the way that he couldn't keep still. His long fingers were at his mouth, he was interlocking his long fingers, or messing with the cuffs of his T-shirt as he expanded on the story that he brought me more than 400 miles to hear. As he talked I said nothing, just looked at him. I took in the short cropped hair. It might be fashionable to have your head almost shaven, but it did this 30 year old mechanic no favours, making him look distinctly aggressive. Even though I'm lucky to not be receding, I can't think of ever wanting to wear my hair that short. Just the opposite. I prefer it collar length.

Not that Mike was any angel; I remember watching him get a little over-enthusiastic in a bar at Monza a couple of years back, avenging a slur made against Damon Hill – who was at that moment thousands of miles away and blissfully unaware of the entire incident – by pulverising an especially mouthy Ferrari fan. It was only the prompt action of the rest of our free-fall drinking squad in spiriting him away through the back door as the carabinieri screeched to a halt at the front of the bar that saved him from being tossed into jail for a few nights.

As I poured us a scotch each from my hip flask, he carried on unfolding his theory. He reckoned that Tel Martin, a man whose ruthlessness had already led to him having far more enemies than friends by a ratio of maybe twenty to one, was bringing in bags of cocaine every month. And he was using the team as cover, which was what had led to Mike deciding that something needed to be done about it.

When I'd first met Mike he was a junior mechanic on Martin's team, Marsport Racing, and it was thanks to my introducing him to Ray that he'd moved on – and up in terms of both status and earning power – to the GTD equipe. As he explained to me, the last thing he wanted was any of his old mates at Marsport getting contaminated in the fall-out if and when Martin was caught in the act. Martin, we both knew, was a devious and conniving bastard, and wouldn't think twice about blaming somebody else. So far as the unlovable Tel was concerned, anybody else is always dispensable.

"The thing is, you're well known" he continued "nobody'd think twice at seeing you around, so I was hoping that you'd see if you can find anything out. Y'know, follow Tel about for a bit and see if he does anything stupid."

"There's no way he'd do anything stupid in sight of anyone, Mike, and you know it. Look, I'm a motorsport writer and photographer, not some News Of The Screws investigative hack. But allright, I'll see if I can find anything. But I'm only going to give it this weekend, and if nothing turns up then I'm back to real life."

Five minutes after he'd gone I was stretched out in the bath, soaking in the foamy water, sipping the last of my drink, and wondering if there was anything to the story. I ought to have been tired to the point of exhaustion – it was almost midnight and I'd been on the road since a little after four that morning – but there was something about the scenario that Mike had unfolded that intrigued me. All I had to do was to find a two-kilo bag of cocaine in Tel Martin's briefcase, get him to confess to being an importer in front of the nearest magistrate, then sell the story to the Sunday Times and the film rights to David Putnam, and I'd have it all sewn up. Sorry, but after running out of whisky at midnight in a pleasant but soul-less hotel in the Kingdom of Fife, that's the nearest I can get to irony.

I felt like I'd been asleep for about ten minutes when the telephone rang, and the lilting voice of a female came down the wire to tell me that it was seven thirty and this was my alarm call. I put the receiver back down, picked up my cigarettes and lighter, and kick-started my system.

The circuit had cranked up a gear when I pulled into the media meadow an hour later; it was Saturday, with qualifying not scheduled to begin until two that afternoon, but even so the public were starting to stream in on their shuttle buses from the park-and-ride fields five miles away. I made a mental note to pay my hotel bill that night, so that I could leave the next morning before the staff came on and get down to the track for about eight. I'd be able to blag a breakfast off some team or other, to compensate for leaving the Inverloch before their kitchen opened. If the Saturday was a guide, then on race day it would be heaving busy and I loathe and detest having to queue to get into race circuits.

A watery sun was beginning to break through the clouds as I sat under the canopy of the GTD motorhome, having tucked into bacon, scrambled egg, sausage, black pudding, beans and sauté potato. I was just spreading marmalade onto my last piece of toast when I spotted Tel Martin striding purposefully along the makeshift lane that had been formed between this row of motorhomes and the ones facing me. He was heading to the paddock, where his pair of race cars would be stood on their jacks being fussed over by the dozen engineers that formed the core of his team. Although a brisk breeze was keeping the ambient temperature on the Scottish side of cool, Martin was apparently unperturbed – his broad, solidly-built five feet six tall frame was wrapped in a crisp white short-sleeved shirt with the team name embroidered on the left sleeve, and a pair of knee-length royal blue chino shorts that matched the piping on his shirt.

"Bit out of your way, isn't it?" he asked me, as he responded to the wave that I'd given as he came into range.

"Yeah, but thought I'd better make the effort." In at the deep end. "I was going to come over and see you later, just to see what's occurring. As I recall I haven't seen you since Silverstone. Kept Missing you at Le Mans."

"Suppose it must be. Why, what do you want to know?" Jesus, was this guy paranoid? Or was it me? If I told any of the other dozen team owners that I wanted to have a chat to get an update, they'd simply say 'yes, when?' or tell me when it suited them to get together. Not Martin, through; this bastard wanted to know why.

"Nothing specific, just a general chat on what's going down."

Martin grunted, looked at his watch, a substantial chunk of Rolex that weighed only slightly less than a housebrick, and re-made eye contact with me. Small, pig-like eyes set into a stubble-chinned face that bore the lines of someone who'd lived hard in his fifty years.

"Come over at four. We'll have finished qualifying then. I can't give you long, though. Ten minutes. That enough?"

"Should be plenty of time, thanks, Tel. See you then."

I watched him disappear along the end of the row of expensive American campers, and turned back to what was left of my breakfast. In the distance an engine suddenly barked, six hundred horsepower crackling into life for the first time that day. No matter how many race days I've attended – and that must by now have run into thousands – there is a still a buzz from hearing four litres of V8 racing engine breathing its first gulps of air and petrol. I drained my coffee, put my head around the door of the kitchen area of the motorhome to thank Annie for the food, and headed for the pits to see what was happening.

At precisely four I tapped on the door of the Marsport motorhome, a forty-foot long shark grey custom-built American beast wearing the near-neon red graphics of Kentucky. The cigarette company was the major, to the point of twenty million dollars a year, sponsor of Martin's pair of low, sleek purpose-built racing coupés. An hour earlier the cars had managed to be fifth and ninth quickest on the day; this meant that the pair of racers would be in with a good chance of a decent result in the two hour race that was the next day's main event. That, I hoped, would have put the Essex-born team owner in a good mood. Tel opened the door, nodded towards the dining table at the far end of the otherwise-deserted luxury mobile home as I stepped inside, and as I settled myself onto the leather-trimmed banquette and placed my MiniDisc recorder and microphone on the light beech-veneered table he joined me, placing two cans of beer down without asking if I'd care for a drink.

When Martin had said ten minutes he'd meant just that – not nine minutes or eleven, but precisely ten. It was long enough for me to be able to determine that Mike was right about the sponsors pulling out. Martin didn't actually say as much, simply that negotiations were in hand and the forthcoming ban on cigarette sponsorship being "a pain in the arse, a load of bollocks from this bloody nanny state." But his edginess suggested that he considered this more than a little local difficulty.

Most of the remaining nine minutes and ten seconds were taken up with Martin's always-opinionated comments about where his cars and drivers were lying in the championship. He added that with four races still to go in the series "you shouldn't write us off yet" as there were still plenty of points in the pot before the circus got to the final round at Magny-Cours, in early October. In short the usual hype that every team supremo trots out at least six times a day throughout the season.

I'd just disengaged my laptop computer from my mobile phone. The newly-finished feature on Will Fellows was e-mailed to London so that it would be waiting for the editor of Auto Racing when he got in on Monday morning. My room phone rang. It was Ray Otley telling me that they were about to stop serving dinner in the restaurant. And that unless I "wanted to starve and use up yet more of their bleedin' food the following morning..." I'd better get my arse into gear. Deciding against changing from the chinos and T-shirt that I'd been wearing all day, I went down as I was. I found myself ordering the set dinner from behind a table that had been hastily rearranged by Ray as soon as he saw me coming down the three steps into the dining room.

The team were in high spirits – they had both of their cars on the front row of the grid for tomorrow's race – and it showed. Not that anybody was drunk, or even slightly inebriated. Racing at this level is a serious business. It costs millions of pounds to put a pair of cars on the grids of all nine rounds of this particular championship, so nobody is going to risk blowing any advantage by nursing a hangover when they are working on the cars during the morning of a race. The buzz was simply the adrenaline surge that comes with stealing an advantage over the rest of the teams. That was all it took to turn the twenty-odd individuals that comprised the GTD team back to their native state of good-humoured hooligans. The only people missing were the drivers; they will have eaten a sensible meal and been packed off to their respective beds early by the paternal Ray, keen to ensure that they are in perfect condition for their work the following morning.

I have no idea what I at that night – it was neither especially good or especially bad – but recall with crystal clarity a conversation that came later as I sat in the plastic oak-beamed bar with Ray, Bill Shepard, his designer, and the team's Chief Engineer, Pat Kearns. The conversation had somehow come around to reincarnation, something that I as neither a practising Buddhist or practising anything else, especially believed in. Pat, his round, open, red face fringed by a thin gingery beard and thinner-still gingery hair, brought the conversation around to my turn.

"If there was anything, or anybody, that you could be when you come back, what would it be?"

"Don't know, it depends how many cracks you get at it. Maybe if I could have lots of different goes at reincarnation I'd spend a few weeks being one of the wasps that hangs around our local bottle bank–"

He jumped straight in, like he does. "Why's that?"

"I could spend the entire month with no responsibilities, pissed for the duration at someone else's expense–"

"But isn't that what you journalists do anyway?"

He had a point. I'd worked out a while back, sat in airport lounge with a half dozen colleagues waiting for our connection back from Milan to Heathrow, that if you were deep enough into this industry and had a sufficiently impressive list of titles to write for, that it would be feasible to live entirely at someone else's expense for months on end. Eating fine foods, drinking good wines and staying in five star hotels around the world, doing no more than picking up a change of clothes every few days and filing copy via a laptop. Maybe Pat was right.

But it wasn't that which made the conversation especially memorable – it was Ray Otley's surprisingly cutting comment about Tel Martin. "I reckon he's already reincarnated..." he'd said. "... he used to be a slug in a former life and decided to come back as Tel because being a slug was too respectable for him."

We all laughed at the time, but thinking back on it later I was slightly chilled; Ray, a man with rarely a bad word to say about anybody, had been, by his standards, seriously cutting; coming from a woman it would have been described as bitchy. From Ray it was even worse, a damning indication of how much a piece of low-life Martin was deemed to be.

The grain of truth that had emerged about Tel Martin's financial situation had sealed it. Although I'd told Mike I'd give it the weekend, I was being sucked into believing that there was more to the story. But I'd better start pulling together some evidence. I lay in bed that night formulating a sketch of action. Not a full-blown plan – I was too tired to do that – but at least a basic outline of what I ought to do.

I resolved to start with some pictures. In most sports, walking around taking photographs of the background crew of an athlete, the support system for a yachting team or whatever would be at best suspicious, and at worst distinctly dangerous. I'd been a sports hack for years and had learned many years ago that no matter how pure and clean it might appear, even the most apparently innocuous sports have seedy underbellies, stones that when you lift them up reveal all manner of obnoxious and loathsome beings. Trying to photograph, say, a boxer's second or an off-duty football manager can lead to a good hiding, as one or two of my former colleagues at Sports World had found out the hard way. One snapper, trying to get a shot of boxer Lennie De Vaughn's manager, had ended up with a broken arm and a Nikon to match. But motor racing was different.

Everybody in racing understands that having their photographs taken by hordes of professionals and thousands of amateurs simply goes with the territory. So in a fifteen minute period and walking no more than half a mile, I'd managed to get two rolls of film shot, all of which featured either the equipment or the people that comprised Marsport. I had the trucks, the tool bays built into the side of the trucks, the spares bay, the workshop canopy, the camper and its awning, and of course a plentiful selection of every member of the team. Using a long zoom lens I was able to get one or two portrait shots of my prime target, Tel, without him being aware that I was on his case. I had no real reason for needing all those shots – it would be a couple of weeks on before I appreciated their value and usefulness – but something told me I ought to get them just the same. You never know...

Knockhill's a narrow, twisty track that bike racers adore. Formula Ford racers like it too, and so do touring car drivers. But compared to the major tracks that the sportscar drivers usually work on, it is tiny. "It's like trying to blast a Formula One car around a kart track" was how Mick Rafferty described the place. So it was no surprise that when the flag dropped and the cars blasted down the straight towards Duffus, a downhill curve that leads right into a left and then another right, there were casualties. Will fellows, starting from the front row, slipped clean away but three cars behind him all tired to take the same piece of track – and Mick Rafferty came off worse, being punted out wide onto the run-off zone and sidewards into the barrier. Seconds later his team-mate was looking at an early bath, too, when he understeered straight into the gravel at the exit of Butchers. Clouds of dust kicked up as Dave Walls's race car ground to a halt, beached and not going anywhere. Form my vantage point looking down onto the curve I watched him extract himself, kick the back tyre of his now-dead Porsche, then begin to trudge up the hill and back to the paddock.

Then the race settled down, the survivors getting into a rhythm that didn't substantially change for the rest of the race.

As expected, Will Fellows got a walk-over win for GTD, bringing the Cosworth-engined race car home almost 27 seconds ahead of the next best entry and extending his and the team's leads in the championships by another handful of vital points apiece. I found this out by tuning my car stereo into the series radio station that was broadcasting a running commentary – by the time that the champagne corks were beginning to pop on the podium I was already approaching the Forth Road Bridge, heading for home. I'd learned years ago that unless there's a damn good reason for staying to the end of a big race then get out ahead of the crowd; the alternative is to be stuck in traffic jams for hours. And anyway, by the time the chequered flag has been waved I've usually long-since finished my work.

Two days of nice weather after Friday's rain had been all it took to get the Sids and their matching Dorises out for the day. All in their

Ladas, Skodas or Honda Civics in search of that elusive thing, the British countryside. There were enough of them pottering along the M74 and the M6 to ensure that despite leaving Knockhill at just before five, it was still after midnight when I finally pulled into the yard at Bennett's Farm. I decided to leave everything exactly where it was in the car, unlocked the door of the caravan, fell inside and within five minutes tumbled into my waiting bed. I hadn't bothered to straighten the duvet when I'd left in the small hours of Friday morning. As Willie Rushton once observed, 'Wasn't your bed the most comfortable place in the world when you got out of it?'

2

Down on the Farm, Oxfordshire

Time has taught me to ignore the cacophony of noise led by Atilla that goes with the territory of a real working farm. Allright, so he's a cockerel, but I couldn't resist nicknaming the leader of Hilda's gang of free-range birds Atilla The Hen. After the luxury of a lie-in until almost eight I rolled out of bed, lit a cigarette and filled the kettle. A beautiful sunny morning was enough to persuade me to take my morning coffee on what I describe as the patio; a small space to the side of the front door. Small, but big enough to take a plastic set of four chairs and a matching table that Alf donated when I'd first moved in three years ago. I looked out across the vivid green of the field on the far side of the lane, towards the woods a half mile or so east. A crow cawed as it passed overhead.

Alf and Hilda are sort of family. When I'd found myself both jobless and homeless after Sports World had gone pear-shaped on me, taking the salary with it, the Bennetts had stepped straight in with the invitation to make long-term use of the caravan that they'd just vacated. They had lived in it for almost a year whilst their farmhouse was being completely renovated. At first I'd demurred, partly because I don't like taking charity and partly because it was in a village a half-dozen miles south-east of Oxford, and I'd got used to living in London. But pragmatism had overcome the first of my thin objections, and the fact that the majority of the motor sport industry is in the same strip of Oxfordshire as the farm overcame the second.

Within two minutes of shooing a large and indolent hen off the table top and sitting down to savour my first drink of the day, Hilda appeared, striding towards me with a large bundle of mail in her hands; three daysworth of press releases and bills. Despite their respective forenames, which I'd always considered to be the familiars given to people who were born already fifty years old, both she and Alf were within two years of my own thirty eight summers. It was just that they both come from the good, traditional, yeoman stock untouched by any tendency towards christening children Donna, Darren, Tracy or anything else modern.

"I've just put some breakfast on for Alf" she declared as she plonked the hefty pile of envelopes down in front of me without even saying hello. "He's over at the wood trying to get rid of some of the stock doves that are massacring the crop in Latchford meadow. If you're nice to me I could make it run to three of us..."

"Thanks, that'd be wonderful. I've nothing in." I responded.

"That'll be the day when you actually have some food in your fridge. If it wasn't for us and the Chinese in Wheatley you'd starve. As soon as Alf appears, come over." with which she was turning on the heel of her trainer and heading back to the main house.

They'd mentioned the possibility of using the caravan to me at Pippa's party, a family 21st celebration that had tempted Alf and Hilda down to London for the day. It was the weekend after I'd been left high and dry by the disappearance of that Italian bastard. Cutreno, Nicolo Cutreno, who's departure had started the house of cards collapse of the publishing house that bore his initials. I hadn't been in much of a party mood; it was only my mother's insistence that forced me into putting in an appearance at the house overlooking Wandsworth Common.

I went up to Oxford later that week, and had been pleasantly surprised by what I found. The caravan was by the side of the yard gate. I'd expected one of those poxy little two-berth things. Those favoured by people who can't bear to be separated from their cornflakes when they hook up a caravan to the back of the family Volvo and toddle off on holiday to Cornwall the first weekend of every August. But I had found a substantial mobile home that was only one step removed from a chalet. It was connected to the mains for water and electricity, had a fully-equipped kitchen with microwave and gas cooker, a telephone line, and sewage via the farm's septic tank. There was a separate lounge and a large double bedroom, and the bathroom was equipped with a seriously good power shower.

Primed by my mother – who I think is Alf's second cousin by marriage – they were aware that I was totally skint. My overdraft was cleared by my salary every month, then built up again to the next pay-day. But suddenly there'd be no more pay-days.

"But I can't afford to rent it off you–"

"Yeah, we know. But the place is empty, and anyway it'll cost us more to move than the place is worth. I'd have to rent a truck and... Anyway, when things turn around you can start chipping in. 'Til then you're welcome to use the place."

"Cheers Alf, that's really good of you."

It had taken almost a year of scratching around to make a living before I could formalise a rent arrangement. Eventually we'd settled on a figure of fifty quid a week all in, except for the telephone which was to be my own responsibility. I couldn't even get a council flat in Brixton for that, let alone somewhere with idyllic views and only five minutes from the M40. I'd have been a fool not to take it. I snapped their hands off.

Anyway, I'd really grown to love the place, not just the caravan but also its location, not much over an hour from London. And less than that to Silverstone, the circuit where I seem to spend a disproportionate amount of my time as it is the main testing facility for most of the race teams whose existence I chronicle in words and pictures. Best of all it's only five minutes from the pub, and handy for a good Chinese takeaway.

After a definitive countryman's breakfast – Alf had been out since five, and was by his own admission "bloody starvin', mate" I was ushered out of the kitchen and ambled back across to the caravan. I checked the answering machine, made three inconsequential calls in response to messages left while I'd been away, and decided to make the effort and clean the place up a bit before starting work.

If truth be told this was a regular thing, for although I had a couple of half-finished pieces in my computer I was in the usual state of apathy that invariably followed a weekend away at a track; I needed to do something therapeutically mindless for a little while before I could get my head around work. The film of grey dust across the top of my CD deck was the deciding factor – that and not being able to find a clean coffee mug.

Once I'd cleared some space in the lounge, which doubles as my office, and emptied the car, I gathered together the rolls of film that I'd shot over the weekend and put them in a plastic bag on the table. Then had a leisurely shower, and dressed properly; as usual, I'd simply pulled on a T-shirt and pair of jogging pants when I'd first dared to greet the morning sun. I drove into Oxford, dropped the rolls into the labs for a one-hour process, and retired to the pub around the corner to read the morning paper and drink a quiet solitary pint while I waited for the technicians to do the business with the dozen Fuji Velvia 135s that I'd left in their care.

The stuff was all good, more to the credit of the equipment I use than to my own abilities through the viewfinder. Looking through the magnifier at each frame over the lightbox on my dining table-cum-desk, I was well pleased with the photographic results of my weekend's work. I took out a half-dozen manila folders out of the part-used pack in the cupboard, marked them up with the names of the features with which they ought to connect, and spent a half hour cutting up the transparency sheets into appropriate collections.

There were two complete rolls, left neatly packaged in the clear carrier sheets that they'd come in from the labs, dedicated to the Marsport team. These included some excellent close-ups of Tel Martin. Looking at these was all it took to bring my train of thought back to the conversations I'd had in Scotland. Although Mike's pleas to investigate Tel Martin were prominent in my train of thought, it was Ray Otley's comments linking Martin and a slug that kept coming back to haunt me. I stretched out on the brown leatherette-covered bench behind the dining table and tried to figure out what to do next.

A day later I was in the office of Auto Racing, trawling through their archive copies with the aid of the index, and collecting photocopies of everything that they had ever published on Tel Martin and his team. It was almost seven when I left there. Chris, the editor, had given me carte blanche to root as deep as I liked and to stay as long as I needed. I'd told him I'd been asked by Racing Publications to think about writing a book on the man and his team. And as I'd arranged to do another archive trawl at another magazine the next morning, I figured that going back to Oxford was second best. Just before starting the car I rang Janice, to see if I could stay over with her that night.

"Jesus, Mark, there's nothing like taking bleedin' liberties" was her initial response, when I suggested this to her. "Lucky for you I'm not working tonight. Where are you now?"

"Richmond."

"Allright lover. See you in an hour or so."

As simple as that. Janice and I'd had an informal arrangement for about five years. If we were both in the same area we'd spend a night together, but she worked nights as an exotic dancer – a stripper on the rugby club and stag party scene, in other words – and I was away most weekends through from April to November. So when the days were long we might only see each other three or four times. Between Christmas and the start of the racing season, when we are both at our least busy, it would maybe increase in frequency to twice a month. As I drove over towards the little terraced house that she owned in Thornton Heath, I realised that it'd been almost six weeks since I'd even spoken to her, and longer still since we'd seen each other. Never mind, the relationship – or maybe that's too grand a term for such an easy and unstructured arrangement – was based on that sort of elasticity.

"The least you can do is take me for an Indian" was the second thing that she said to me, the first being that I was bang out of order for not having picked the phone up in bleedin' months.

The racing scene is a gloriously large scale singles club, not of the 'let's get fixed up' variety, but simply a gathering together of an awful lot of people who spend their weekends away from homes and partners. Sometimes fresh relationships can blossom, although in a working world when most of the females are usually public relations staff or caterers this is relatively rare. For starters, they're outnumbered ten to one by males. And I was one of that ninety percent who'd never developed anything with any females working at the track.

Once I'd started to talk to them, the only ones I'd ever shown any interest in had turned out to be either bimbos or balls crushers. And anyway, about the last thing I want to talk about when I'm trying to relax is work – so my friendship with an extraordinarily attractive girl who happens to make two hundred quid a night from taking her clothes off is, to me, sensible. She's got no interest at all in motor sport, and has a wonderfully ability to pick up and re-tell fascinating tales. She's altogether good fun to be around.

She can also be awesomely outrageous. One time we'd been for a meal in a quite nice little French place near Covent Garden, an evening which was in danger of being spoiled by staggeringly indifferent service from the surly, almost belligerent staff.

"This is gettin' bleedin' stupid" she'd announced, after we'd spent more than twenty minutes trying to order another bottle of wine. At which she stood up and slowly began to unbutton the shirt that she was wearing. She'd just revealed the second of her wonderfully-shaped, bra-free breasts ("all mine, you know" she'd declared to me one night in the privacy of her bedroom. "No bleedin' silicon here…") and brought the entire eating public to a slack-jawed halt when the maitre d' came over, eyes fixed firmly on her naked dark brown pointed nipples, spluttering something incoherent in French. This clearly was something that didn't happen very often in La Belle Époque.

"We'd like another bottle of house red. Please." was all that Janice had said, and immediately started to fasten up her buttons again. Sitting down she fixed me with an impish smile – blissfully aware of the fact that every eye in the room was still on her, but totally indifferent to the attention – and commented "That got his bleedin' attention, dinnit?" and resumed eating.

Best of all, the bottle of Vin de Pays that arrived two minutes later in the hands of the maitre d' – his eyes still preferring to dwell on Janice's chest rather than making eye contact – was "avec nous compliments, Mademoiselle…"

I'd never seen her at work – although I had a pretty good idea of what she could offer to an attentive audience, thanks to occasional private views – nor did I have any real desire to. I was quite content to see her as and when it suited us both, and to get on with my own life in between. After a typically enjoyable night, and with a promise to ring her again soon, I was back in my car and heading for the West End offices of Motorsport News, the other magazine that I'd already arranged to visit, to get copies of whatever they'd published about Tel Martin over the years.

3

Does it make sense?

It was late afternoon when I pulled back into the yard, waving to Alf – who was busy at the door of an outbuilding doing whatever it is that farmers do to their tractors – as I parked up. His dog Shep yapped a couple of times, then bounded over to me for some fuss. Once he'd had enough and plodded back across to guard Alf, I went indoors and started work.

During my two days in London I'd accumulated a pile of A4 paper that was almost six inches high. By the time that I'd completed my initial collate-and-read session I knew everything I needed to know about the public history of Tel Martin.

I'd started with both piles of papers, the one culled from the pages of Auto Racing and the others taken from the archives of Motorsport News, and as I read I merged them into one pile with the oldest material at the top. There was a considerable degree of duplication – inevitable when two journalists are reporting on the same event – but there were also more personalised impressions. Especially in the later reports which had benefited from the relaxation in reporting style that had tiptoed in during the seventies.

I broke off as soon as the last pages were in place, poured a beer, and mulled over what I had learned. There was little that was news to me, but there was enough to make me far more intimately grounded about Marsport and about Martin himself than previously.

The first mention of him came from Motorsport News in the middle of 1969, when he was tipped as One To Watch following his first win in a saloon car racing event. He was then 22, had been born in Grays, Essex, and worked at the family Vauxhall garage. I scribbled down a note to see if the dealership was still in existence and to check it out when I asked my old friend Paul to go to Companies House, after which I would hopefully have more on Martin's business activities.

During the course of the next five years Martin had become increasingly prominent, having moved up to the British Touring Car

Championship where he carved his way into the record books by scoring a total of eight wins. He had also raced in the 24 Hour race at Le Mans, and the similar event at Spa during 1974, racing a Porsche.

By 1976 the mentions of Tel Martin as a racing driver had gone, to be replaced by those for Marsport. This was a team which had been formed to run a racing Ford Escort, with Paul Shears driving. He'd moved his team up the ladder to race in Touring Cars with a variety of different cars – and equally varied results – throughout the rest of the Seventies. Then in 1981 he shifted up another gear into Sports Car Racing.

These machines are a world apart from showroom sports cars; they are low, sleek, very fast and hugely expensive machines that are only vaguely related to production cars from whatever manufacturer whose badge might appear on their bonnets. Viciously powerful tools, they are designed to hit more than 220 miles an hour on the Mulsanne straight at the sport's spiritual home of Le Mans, and to cover an entire 8.5 mile lap of that same circuit at an average speed on the high side of 145 miles an hour.

It takes big money just to race at Le Mans each summer, and if you decide to enter the rest of the Championship then you can cube the amount of cash that you'll need in the bank. From 1981 right through to this season Tel Martin's team had been bankrolled by Euro-American Tobacco, but from what I'd learned that would all end once the final flag is dropped at the end of this season. Which would leave Tel with a major problem.

People like Tel will go to virtually any length to get the cash together to go racing. They see the team's performance as an extension of their own virility, if you were to believe the crap written by a psychologist a couple of years ago. And if what Mike'd told me was true, in the case of Marsport the ultimate length involves importing kilogramme packs of a Class A drug on a wholesale level. How the fuck'll he manage to translate that to a logo on the side of his car? The Coca Cola Corporation has already bagged '*Things Go Better With Coke*' so that one's out of the frame...

I spent the next few hours organising the list of public achievements of Tel Martin in his various roles within the sport, keying them into the computer as I went through the pile of sheets. At a little after midnight I printed out a copy, and put it in the same folder as the set of transparencies that I'd shot at Knockhill.

I backed up all of the new files onto a high-capacity disk, locked this away in the small fireproof safe that I'd acquired for this purpose two years ago, and shuffled off to bed. I'd tidy up the rest of the debris in the morning. Or not, depending on how I felt.

I didn't bother tidying up. Instead I spent all of Thursday and the first half of Friday hacking out the rest of the pair of unfinished features that had been hanging over me since the previous week (prompted by a call from the section editor of the Sunday newspaper for whom the first piece was destined) then got into the car and drove down to London, where I'd arranged to meet Paul in a pub off Fetter Lane to pick up the microfiche files that he'd obtained on my behalf from Companies House.

"He's got all sorts" said Paul, as we sat working our way through the first pint of Directors' Bitter in the Lamb and Flag's busy bar area. "He's got seventeen companies – which reminds me, you owe me forty eight quid plus vat, cash'll do nicely – and I've got copies of all their returns. A couple of them are dormant, but the rest are active. Everything you need's in here. How will you read them? You haven't got a fiche reader have you?" he concluded, handing me a bulky legal-weight brown envelope.

"No, but I've a pal who owns a car dealership and they have one in the spares department that they don't use anymore. They're on CD-Rom these days for parts lists. He lets me borrow a corner of the stores and use that whenever I need to read one."

I had known Paul since college days. We had gone through school together, being pals without being especially friendly, but once we'd moved up to Dorset College we found ourselves attending the same lectures, then started to drink together. We'd kept in touch beyond there. He moved into accountancy and I'd fallen from family grace by declining to get involved in my father's granary business. Instead I became a local newspaper reporter.

These days he has a partnership in a business in the heart of the City, and we tend to get together from time to time for a pint. Whenever I needed anything sorting, from forming a company to avoid paying tax to getting some background material needed on the activities of some individual or company, it was Paul Laker that I rang. He never needed to find anything out through me, but the one-way exchange of information – for which I invariably paid no more than it had cost him – never affected our friendship. The nearest I'd got to returning the compliment was by taking him and his business partner to a couple of big races at Silverstone; thanks to my connections I'd been able to get them into the British Racing Drivers Clubhouse, which they appreciated as the rare treat it was.

It took me more than half of Saturday to go through the microfiche sheets. Not a great problem to me, but hassle to the lads in the parts store, under whose feet I was for this period. These tiny images, stored in clusters on 5" pieces of acetate film, were copies of the many forms that are statutorily filed at Companies House by every limited company in Great Britain. Romantically titled sheets of paper such as 288b, or Forms 10 or 12, they give information on the directors, on the shareholders, a copy of the most recent trading accounts, and the address of the company. I had filled in a quarter of an A4 legal pad with scribbling by the time I'd finished reviewing the films, and all I knew as I drove back home to try and start working out precisely what I'd learned was that Paul was right – Tel Martin had his fingers in a lot of pies.

As expected, the prominent names were Terence Charles Martin and Lianne Martin, both of Dean House, Dean Hollow, Epping, Essex. The primary company from my point of view was Martin Industries (Motorsport) Limited, with a registered office in Braxted, Essex. But the shareholding in that company was registered to MMI Trust Limited of Douglas, Isle of Man.

I worked out that all but one of Martin's seventeen businesses were registered as having overseas shareholdings. Not unknown, and a neat way of treading the fine line between tax avoidance and tax evasion. The exception was the family car dealership (the continuing existence of which I'd been wondering about...) which listed not just Tel and his wife Lianne, but also one Diane Winfield, of another Epping address, as shareholders. She and Tel, but not Lianne, were listed as directors of that company.

My brain was beginning to ache by the time I finished plodding through my notes and putting them into a basic database on the computer. So I took my usual escape route and walked threequarters of a mile along the lane to the Marquis of Granby. My local watering hole, an isolated thatched inn dating back to another world. To its one cream-painted room where five pints of the wonderful amber liquid produced by Hook Norton Brewery awaited my attentions.

It was wonderful to have the luxury of a summer weekend at home. As tends to happen around British Grand Prix time the rest of the major National series take a short break, so I had no Touring Car meeting to attend, and the next round of the Sportscar Series was not until two weekends hence. The GP was still a week away – although I'd need to get myself over to Silverstone on Thursday and be there each of the next three days, getting to the track earlier each successive day to avoid the crowds – and I made the most of my free time by relaxing. This ranged from having lazy mornings through to protracted periods playing my electric guitar.

A couple of years ago, about twenty years later than most of my friends, I had decided to take up playing the guitar more seriously. Flushed with the success of the first – surprisingly big – royalty cheque from the book on an F1 racing driver that I'd written in the first few months after moving to Oxfordshire, I bought myself a vintage sunburst red Fender Stratocaster guitar and a Marshall amplifier. Until then my sum abilities at playing the guitar were drawn from a Bert-Weedon-play-with-yourself-in-three-days tutorial book, making use of a cheap acoustic, little more than a few pieces of plywood with strings attached. But suddenly there I was with a guitar that looked just like the one that Eric Clapton uses.

Move over Eric, and I'll show you how its done.

It hadn't, of course, worked out anything like that, but what I lacked in skill I more than made up for in enthusiasm, and when really concentrating could turn out a tolerable, if stilted and unflowing, version of the sassy bit from *Stairway To Heaven.* I spent three hours plodding away at learning to recreate the lead part from Lynyrd Skynyrd's *Freebird,* only stopping when Hilda put her head around the door of the caravan and suggested that I give it a rest because the chickens would stop laying if I carried on. I pulled a face at her, unplugged the guitar and propped it back up in the corner, switched off the amplifier, and opened my laptop computer.

Back to the real world and see if there was any mileage in this story about Tel Martin. I flicked open my personal organiser, found Mike Lewis's number, and rang him. Like me, he would be enjoying a Sunday off.

Fancy a pint?"

"For sure. No car, though. Can you pick me up?"

I collected him up outside his home an hour later, and drove to the Bell, just down the road from where he lives in Banbury.

"Cheers." I acknowledged the fact that he'd bought the first pint, before relaying the conversation that I'd already had in my head. "I've taken a look around Tel's business, checked out the companies that he's got. But there's nothing iffy at all. He has most of his money stashed overseas in the Isle of Man, but there's nothing illegal in that. The racing team is profitable – but not by a huge amount – and he's got a house in Epping. I've not been able to find out if he owns it outright, and I haven't been able to find out what the score is with his workshops, either. The fact is, on the strength of what I've seen so far he's up to nothing iffy. You know what the score is..." I continued "I can't afford to keep chasing round after Martin in the hope that something'll turn up. I need to make a living. I told you I'd give it a bit of thought and I have but–"

"But you told Ray you were supposed to be writing a book about Tel Martin."

"Cover. Telling him that was a good way of covering questions."

Mike looked crestfallen. Then his face brightened again. "So why don't you do a book about him? That way you could follow him around a lot and still get paid for it."

There was a certain logic to Mike's suggestion. But the big questions which hung over me as I worked my way gradually through the one pint of bitter that I'd allocated myself (Driving doesn't half screw up my drinking...) were One, would I be able to get Barrington to go with the idea of a book on this particular character, and Two, would I want to do it anyway, even in Martin agreed to being the subject of a permanent record of his life? Nothing happened in the rest of the hour that I spent with Mike to resolve these two linked issues. All I got were reiterations of his conviction that Tel Martin was bringing drugs into the country, and that he expected me to sort it all out.

Barrington Rutherford was, as usual, not expected in until after eleven. At about five past my telephone rang. "Hello old love, gather you called. We don't owe you any royalties, do we? Didn't think the next lot were due before the end of September." Barry's plummy old-school voice, its rich and mellifluous tones proof of the expensive education that he'd concluded some thirty years previously, came oozing out of the handset.

"No, but if there're any going, I'd appreciate them, or more to the point my bank manager would. No, the reason for the call is that I've had an idea for a book that I thought I'd like to run by you."

Five minutes later, having outlined my proposed new book, I had an agreement; I'd have to deliver the book by the end of the year for next Spring's list, and there would be a contract and a small advance on royalties in the post to me by the end of the week. I'd already put three books out through Barry's company and an agreement to come up with something new was an easy, simple process. No need to get into heavy negotiations and start producing a synopsis; a simple call was all it took to get the go-ahead.

I put the phone down once I'd finished talking with Barry and two minutes later was on to Marsport's offices in Essex. After listening for thirty seconds or so to *A Lover's Concerto* being played by what sounded like a tone-deaf Turkistani harpist playing with his instrument in the bathroom, I was put through to Tel.

"Why me? Where's the story?" True to form and entirely as expected,

Tel Martin was deeply suspicious. I launched into the script I'd got ready and waiting in my mind about him being one of the most interesting and colourful characters on the international racing scene for several decades, and how I'd been persuaded by my publishers that there was a story to tell. Punctuated only by occasional grunts, I spent almost five minutes trying to win Tel over to the idea. I eventually managed this by assuring him that he would have final approval of the text before it was published – I knew that I'd succeeded by an audibly underwhelmed "Allright, then" from my target. Two hurdles jumped neatly in ten minutes.

But a couple of grand in advance wouldn't go very far – I'd have to slot all of the work on the book into the loose and unstructured schedule that I had stretching out in front of me from there to the end of the season. Which, for the immediate future, involved schlepping over to Silverstone for several days, for the occasion of the British Grand Prix. I had a couple of specific briefs for this; to get interviews with a young Czech driver for a German magazine and with Peter Lawrence of the eponymous racing team for an executive lifestyle monthly. But with a bit of luck I'd also be able to come up with a couple of flyers, stories that just unfolded during the course of the weekend.

The Lawrence piece was quick and easy to get together; I'd first met Pete a decade ago and had already arranged to meet him in his motorhome on Thursday evening, after the day's work was finished. In the course of a relaxed forty minutes I'd got everything new that I needed – I already had his background on file back at home which would provide any missing bits.

But if talking with Pete was a breeze, Radavan Caryzich proved the exact opposite. Hampered by three factors – his knowledge of colloquial English has yet to rise above minimal, he kept looking at his watch every three minutes clearly wanting to be somewhere, anywhere, else, and that he is a brilliant driver with no apparent external interests – it is no wonder that he gives the impression of being the world's most boring person. If pushed for a quickfire description of him, I'd have to say that he's a multi-millionaire train spotter in a flash baby-grow suit.

Back in the good old days before corporate sponsors started calling the shots racing drivers used to race hard and party harder; today they are more likely to go out and paint the town beige. These guys might do the most exciting job in the world, but with only isolated exceptions you'd get more stimulus from sitting in a hotel room in rural Albania reading the notes that come with your annual tax return.

I was just passing through the security gate heading for coffee in the media centre when I bumped into Tel Martin. He was in a shirt provided by the Delta-Ford team, the same people who had invited him as a weekend guest and who had provided him with the Access All Areas pass that was swinging nonchalantly from a navy blue cord around his thick-set neck. He blasted me with a disarmingly sincere smile as he caught sight of me struggling to squeeze my camera bag through the narrow turnstile.

"Beer?" The word was a question, and invitation and a command all wrapped up in four letters.

I nodded in agreement, did a full lap of the chrome-plated turnstile at the entrance to the paddock – getting my bag snagged up again, to the amusement of the security guard – and doubled back to where the motor homes were parked.

Tel was in a chatty mood as we headed towards the Delta Winnebago. He talked virtually non-stop as we traversed the hard concrete of the paddock and wove through the crowds of engineers, mechanics and dozens of other people, delivering his opinion on the top half-dozen players. He'd just tipped Schumacher, Ferrari's top gun, for the win, when we walked up the steps into the motor home. He led me in there as though he owned the place – but then he almost did, at one time.

If he hadn't been born of East End Jewish parents or if Paul Dell, the senior director of Delta Formula One hadn't gone, successfully, in search of Arab oil money to fun the team's racing a dozen years ago, Tel would almost certainly have been running the operation today. As it was he'd become a willing casualty for the greater good. Nobody had ever quite figured out the relationship between Martin and Dell. It was known that they'd been flat-mates for a while, and one of the more entertaining rumours that surfaced from time to time was that they had both been getaway drivers during the near-legendary Piccadilly Bullion Robbery back in the mid-seventies. But rumours like that were all part of the folk-lore of the racing scene anyway so nobody paid that much attention.

All of which I was to ponder over a couple of days later, lying on the padded bench in my caravan back at the farm. The telephone rang. It was a policeman, an Inspector Granville, inviting me to pop down to the station in Oxford and help them with their enquiries into the sudden death of Mike Lewis. Only they didn't tell me he was dead at that point.

4
An Inspector Calls

"Are you a friend of Michael Lewis?' The Inspector, who had introduced himself as Granville, sat opposite me and extended the hand holding a lit match as he asked. I drew on my cigarette and looked him in the eye.

"Yeah, we've known each other for a couple of years. Why?"

"Just trying to work out a few things. Would you go through what you've done together over the past few days, please Mr McDermott?"

"But what's happened to him?"

"I'm sorry, we aren't at liberty to say yet, sir. Would you mind filling us in with what happened, when you saw him, why, and where?"

"He rang me last week and asked if I'd be going to the Grand Prix. I told him of course. I'd be going every day from Thursday through to Sunday. He asked if I'd mind taking him on Saturday and Sunday. He was working until Friday but'd like to go for qualifying and the race. But his car was knackered. So I picked him up early on Saturday, gave him a lift to the track, and dropped him home again that night. I did the same again on Sunday."

"And what time did you drop him off? I take it you did drop him at home on Sunday night...?"

"Yeah, about One in the morning."

"Wasn't that rather late? I watched the race on television and it was all over by four. What did you do for the other nine hours?"

"Have you ever tried getting out of Silverstone after the Grand Prix?" I held steady eye contact with my inquisitor. "Anyway, I was invited to the post-race party at Jordan Racing, it's the high spot of the weekend. And I managed to get Mike an invite. We left there at about midnight, and got straight out of the track."

"And you went straight home after dropping your friend off? And is there anybody that can confirm your going straight home?"

"Yes, I went straight home. And it's possible that the Bennetts might have heard my car – sometimes they do, sometimes they don't. Anyway, what is all this about?"

"In a moment, Sir. Do you have a telephone number for them? and who are the Bennetts, anyway? Do you live with them?"

I explained my domestic arrangements and gave them the number of the farmhouse. The other policeman in the room scribbled this down and left through the doorway back out into the corridor.

The questioning – in a chatty disguise but questioning nevertheless – continued whilst the junior policeman was presumably checking out my story.

"So how do you know Mr Lewis?"

"I met him a couple of years ago. I'd been at Brands Hatch for a meeting and was just about to leave when a friend asked if I'd mind giving one of his mechanics a lift home. Mike. His Mum had been taken ill. "

"Very good of you. Especially as his home is a good twenty miles further on from where you live."

"Not really, I do about forty thousand miles a year, so another half hour isn't much of an issue to me. And I was glad of the company to be quite honest, it made a change not to be stuck on my own on the M25. I'd already seen him around the tracks so it wasn't as if he was a complete stranger."

"And you've been friends since?"

"Not friends exactly, more acquaintances really. I don't exactly socialise with him as such but we have the odd pint together. Anyway, you still haven't told me what it's all about. Is he in trouble or something?"

"Like I said, I'm not at liberty to say, yet, sir."

We sat in silence for a few minutes, during which I wondered what Mike'd been up to. I knew he wasn't well off, but he seemed able to keep paying the rent on his place and never seemed to be stuck for the price of a round so couldn't figure out why he'd need to get involved in any crime. I knew he could spark off and thump somebody, just like he had in Italy. But would that be enough to get him into serious trouble? My thoughts were interrupted by the second CID officer coming back into the room. He moved in close and said something in a low voice to Granville.

"Mrs Bennett says that she remembers hearing your car at about half past one on Sunday night."

"So now that you have confirmed what I've told you will you tell me what Mike's been up to, and why you asked me here?"

Granville looked across to his colleague – who had never been formally introduced but had simply arrived in the small, cream-painted interview room half a minute behind Granville and me – and then turned back to me, as I stubbed out my cigarette butt into the cheap, pressed aluminium ashtray. Then he spoke.

"I'm afraid that Mr Lewis is dead, sir. He was found this morning in the entry behind his house."

Mike? Dead? I was horrified. Why? How? Who? Granville paused for a moment, registering the look on my face.

"We are given to understand that he was killed at some time between five and six yesterday morning, and one of his neighbours told us that he was out walking his dog when he saw Mr Lewis get out of a car that matched the description of yours at the weekend. Clever chap, even remembered some of the registration number. That's how we found you. Can you think of any reason why he should be out at that time? And who might be responsible?"

Immediately, involuntarily, repulsively, the image of Tel Martin's face flashed across my mind. I couldn't think of anyone else who'd want Mike dead. Had Tel worked out that Mike had heard the rumours about The drug deals and had started talking? Yeah, if anybody would be responsible, if there was anyone to blame, it would be Tel. But he probably didn't do it himself. Probably not his style; too messy. But he could have a hand in it somewhere, be pulling strings from a position of relative safety. "Sorry, no, can't think of anyone who'd want to harm Mike."

There'd be nothing but hassle if I mentioned Tel Martin at this stage. Maybe later?

Stretched out later on the cushioned bench of the caravan, I was drinking a coffee. An image of Mike lying in a pool of blood in a back alleyway dominated my thoughts. I had been stuck for another hour at the police station – and got a parking ticket for overstaying my meter bay into the bargain – before being ushered out of the back entrance. Granville and the other detective hadn't told me any more about Mike's demise, they had just carried on double-checking the detail of my story before apparently reaching a state of satisfaction.

I recalled seeing some retired policeman on the telly. He'd said the last person to see a victim alive is probably the murderer – a bleedin' obvious observation. I'd managed to convince them that I wasn't that last person. What I couldn't figure out was where Tel Martin fitted into this scenario. Mike hadn't let his suspicions go any further than me – had he? – so what grounds had Martin to kill Mike? Or at least give the order to have him killed? Or maybe it was my distaste for what Tel Martin was up to, colouring my thoughts. Maybe it was somebody else entirely. Maybe he'd got into an argument with a neighbour. Maybe he'd gone to get a bit of blow and it'd all gone wrong. Could be anything. I dozed off with a whirl of thoughts coming and going through my mind.

The phone woke me, Ray Otley wondering what I knew about Mike's murder. I ran through my interrogation at the police station, explaining that apart from that he probably knew about as much as I did.

"They'd asked me about it all too, mate. But like you, I haven't a clue why he should have been killed let alone who..."

"Same here, Ray. So why'd they pull you in?"

"They came here to the factory. Wanted to know if he'd been into work Monday–"

"And had he?"

"That's the strange thing. No. First time in I don't know how long that he's not turned in. And his phone was just ringing out when we called him."

By the time that Ray had hung up I was still no wiser, with no more of a clue to why Mike should have been out in the alley behind his house a day and a half after I dropped him off. And why he should have been killed. I was a long way from being sure that it was down to Tel Martin, but I wasn't any closer to being able to figure out any another suspects either. I flicked on the kettle, the stereo and the laptop. Better do a bit of work.

The sound of somebody filling a bottle bank woke me. I leaned across to the bedside table and peered at the alarm; a quarter past bloody five. I went into the bathroom and splashed water onto my face, then went back into my room and looked down onto the avenida a dozen floors below. A solitary police car was speeding down towards the Parc de Mar with siren howling and blue lights flashing. There was nothing else in sight.

It would be a couple of hours before I could even get breakfast, so I went for a shower and pulled on some clothes. It was just starting to come light.

I switched on my laptop and worked for a while, finishing off an article for the tyre company that had kindly flown me out here for the Barcelona round of the Championship. And put me in the five star luxury of this noisy hotel. By ten I was leaning over the barrier alongside the service road at the Circuit de Cataluña, watching the first runners in free practice with a hot late summer sun warming my back and dust blowing onto my legs.

By four thirty that afternoon the GTD team had racked up not just another win, but the driver's championship as well. As the flag was waved at the end of the formation lap Will Fellows had shot ahead of the pack, hurtling forward as though his car had been fired from a slingshot. Just like Mark Knopfler can make playing his National guitar look so damned easy, so it is with Will in a race car; the illusion of consummate ease masks a lifetime of experience. He was never headed, and ran an uneventful race. A stop for fuel was dealt with cleanly, and there was never any threat of losing his commanding lead. Paul Williams fared less well. On the opening lap he went into the Elf curve sandwiched on either side by a pair of Porsches.

Faced with the choice of being crushed as the curve tightened or backing off, he eased the throttle. That was all it took to unstick his car's cold tyres and he skittered onto the slippery rumble strip. Then over it. He slid across the cat litter , kicking up clouds of dust and spinning into the tyre wall. Shards of carbon fibre bodywork flew up on impact, but the door was kicked open and Williams emerged, pulled off his helmet and kicked petulantly at the side of the car as the marshals arrived. I tried to find him later but he was in the motorhome, sulking, waiting for his flight out. He never liked talking much at the best of times, and instinct told me this was a long way from being the best of times. Anyway, I'd got enough shots of him losing to make the trip worthwhile.

I watched as Will bounced around the podium on a wellspring of adrenaline when he was presented with not just the race winner's trophy, but also the laurel wreath that signified his champion status. Three magnums of Moët sprayed like hyperactive lawn sprinklers, and Ray Otley moved around behind his driver to raise will on his shoulders. The rest of the GTD team, everybody from the gopher who polishes the driver's crash helmets to the tyre technicians, even Annie the caterer, whooped and yelped with delight right in front of the podium as they shared a moment of mutual triumph.

An hour after the race wrapped up I was waiting in the paddock for the bus that would take me back to catch my flight to Heathrow. I was still waiting more than an hour later, watching the circus being packed away into its gleaming trucks when Peter appeared at my side.

"You still here? The bus went a few minutes ago..."

"Shit. I was told by the driver he'd see me here at five–"

"Ah. Should I organise a cab for you? I'm here until morning but I can get a car to take you back to the airport..."

One arrived a few moments later. I got to the check-in desk four minutes after the flight had closed.

"There is another flight at 22:30 señor, would you like me to seat you on that?" It was the best offer I could get from the dragon at the desk. I walked out of the terminal and decided to take a cab back into the city and grab a decent meal rather than sit out the next four hours in the lounge.

I found a tapas bar on the edge of the Olympic Village and ordered some food. Small dishes of Patatas Riojanos, squid, chorizo in tomato sauce, bread and a salad of tomato and onion. While I waited for it to arrive I settled into my booth, reading Chris Hilton's biography of Gerhard Berger. I was halfway through my second glass of wine when a familiar voice filtered through the sudden lull in background noise that followed the television being turned off.

"We'll be allright, trust me."

"How? With Kentucky pulling out next month–"

"Trust me. You just carry on with next year's cars, and bring the fuckin' test programme up to speed earlier than this year. If we hadn't started the season a month behind everybody else we'd–"

"But–"

"No excuses. Just make sure the cars are ready to start testing at Estoril after the Christmas break."

The voices were coming from the next booth. I couldn't see them because of the height of the dark wood petitions that isolated each table – and they couldn't see me either. But I'd know Tel Martin's voice anywhere, and I could tell from its tone that he wasn't impressed with the way his cars had trailed in towards the back of the pack during the afternoon. I was still finishing off the last of my chorizo when I heard Tel ask for "la cuenta por favor".

So how was he going to be sure of funding for next season? There was no word of fresh money coming into the series from anywhere, and just about everybody else had declared their sponsorship details for the next season even before the cars had seen the light of day. So he hadn't poached anything. Then an image of Mike lying in a pool of his own blood flashed through my mind and I was right back to base with the drug money connection.

"Make sure that the second rig is at the truck stop on the N33 on the seventeenth at eight at night."

"What?"

"Just make sure it's there... Thanks, yes, that's fine..." Tel was interrupted by the waiter bringing the credit card slip back. "Drive it yourself."

"But–"

"Just do it. He'll be there to meet you."

"But how do I make sure I'm drivi–"

"You'll think of something. Geoff'll have to have an accident or something."

I could hear movement as they got themselves together and left, walking straight away from me without glancing in my direction. I knew Martin and his team manager Paul Stevenson, but I didn't recognise the other man. He'd said nothing and was dressed in a black leather jacket and grey trousers; normal clothes rather than the sponsor-provided leisurewear that acts a uniform for those active in the racing industry. He walked with the kind of limp that old bikers often have. Harley Leg, it's called by the Hell's Angels, in tribute to one too many accidents involving a chrome-plated iron horse.

There was nothing else, no argument. I'd have to get myself to Spa next month, and see what I could find out. I was stretched out across the bed, and Atilla had already kicked off even though it still hadn't started to come light. The plan had been to skip going to Belgium, to get on with some of the other things I had in the pipeline instead. Nothing major was expected at Spa and I could get away with playing truant from the occasional round.

I nursed a tumbler half full of brandy and wound down after the drive back from Heathrow, cursing the extra two hour delay on my flight back from Barcelona. We hadn't even taken off until almost one in the morning. I'd looked out for Tel and his team at the airport, but there'd been no sign of them in the lounge; presumably they'd made their own arrangements, probably the private charter jet that Kentucky makes available from time to time.

I'd seen Will Fellows in the duty free shop and congratulated him on the day's win and his championship. I promised to join him and the team for a drink to celebrate later in the week. Then I went up to the executive lounge, a perk of being flown Club Class. Will, picking up his own flight costs, was flying cattle so I didn't see him again until I was walking through the baggage hall at Heathrow, and spotted him waiting by the carousel for his holdall.

"I hear you're writing a book on Tel Martin."

"Yeah, that's right. How'd you know that?"

"You know what this game's like. You know I drove for Tel a couple of times, don't you?"

"Yeah, long time ago though, wasn't it? When you were still in Formula–"

"If you need anything about that period I might be able to–"

"Cheers Will, I'll call you once I start into the project properly. For now I've got the last couple of rounds to get through. The book's my winter job."

Then he looked at his watch and was gone. In truth I'd completely forgotten about Fellows having worked for Martin, but didn't let him know that. Part of the game is to give these guys the impression that I know everything. The chances of him ever coming up with anything new about Tel would be slim, but I'd talk to him about it at some point, just in case.

I bumped into the head honcho from Kentucky a week after I got back from Spain. We were both at the Dorchester, at an awards dinner run by one of the magazines I sometimes write for, and we'd headed for the lavatories at the same time. I recognised him from the paddocks at race meetings, and introduced myself as a soon as we both had free hands, asking if he could spare me a couple of minutes.

That quiet huddle in the lobby of the hotel provided me with two pieces of vital information. One was that he was about to retire, and the other was that they were pulling out of not just motorsport, but all sponsorship activities in Europe. In his southern drawl he'd explained that the world was a changing place and that they were getting out before they were forced to by incoming legislation. And he was off to breed racehorses in Lexington "...until the sun goes down."

I also felt slightly cheated. Despite his title of President he never bothered to wear the full dress uniform that you'd expect to go with that status (loads of gold spaghetti around rim of a peaked cap, fringed epaulettes, a chestful of medals and ribbons, the full Idi Amin look) but preferred to wear jeans with cowboy boots and an embroidered shirt open at his scrawny tortoise neck. This was a bit odd, because everybody else was in dinner suits. He went back to the large round table that he was sharing with the Marsport crowd – with Tel holding court as expected – and I returned to my own seat, back to my hooligan hack pals across the far side of the room.

Tel Martin had ignored me all night. But later, after the party had all but fizzled out and I was sat alone in the bar nursing a night-cap brandy and a coffee, he joined me.

"How's the book going?"

"I'm still in the early research stages. I won't actually get anything down on paper until the end of the seas–"

"What research?" He cut in with his usual impatience.

"Y'know, the usual, trawling through back issues of mags that have run items on you... that sort–"

"Have you got a publisher?"

"Course. I don't start anything until–"

"Oh yeah, I remember. So when do you need to talk to me again?"

I thought for a second, hoping he was getting the impression of me flicking through the pages of some mental diary. "How are you immediately after the next round, at Spa?"

"Can't, got to get straight back after the race then we're straight off for a week in the Canaries and back in time for France... But after that, give me a ring and we'll get something sorted." And with that he stood, nodded, and left the bar. He hadn't had a drink, and I was left with the impression that he had sought me out.

And he would be getting straight out of Belgium after the flag dropped. Convenient.

The ten days between getting home from the Dorchester and driving onto the ferry on Thursday morning before the race went in a blur. I finished off a couple of pieces that were needed for magazines, spent a drunken night at the GTD workshops on Thursday, and knocked out a little profile of Will for a yearbook. Then I headed down to home for the weekend of Mum's sixtieth birthday. I'd toyed with the idea of taking Janice with me, just for the hell of it, but decided not to. My Mum might not understand that we were just pals, not a partnership. I gave her a call anyway, and left it that I'd see her in London after I'd done the Spa race.

It seemed that no sooner had I got back from Dorset and sorted out a few bits and pieces, booked myself into a Belgian Novotel near the circuit and made an attempt at tidying the caravan, than it was time to drive down to catch the six o'clock boat. The mournful wail of a Willie Nelson track played on the stereo as I rolled through the night down the motorway towards Dover. An appropriate soundtrack to what was always a flattening time as the series wound its way into another winter break with nobody having anything left to prove.

5

Belgium sans frontieres

Instead of taking the AutoRoute direct to Liége and then on to Spa, I came out of Zebrugge, headed down the coast to Ostend and turned east on to the N33. I wanted to check out the truckstop, see the lay of the land there. What I found was a large expanse of smooth tarmac, with a shop and café attached to the side of the filling station. There were a couple of dozen trucks parked up, but the place was huge; it could take ten times that number of artics and still have space to spare. Around the outside edge, alongside the perimeter fence, were marked out spaces for cars. With a bit of luck I ought to be able to bag one of those on Sunday night.

I pulled out of the truckstop, rejoined the road, and turned back around at the first roundabout to aim for Liége.

Even with this diversion I was still in the circuit press office by early afternoon, adding the last laminate of the season to the set of passes swinging in a corded pouch around my neck. I sat at a bar in the infield with a baguette jambon and a large French-style bowl of coffee, wondering what it is that I like best about Spa Francorchamps. The series of demanding bends that make drivers work harder than almost anywhere else? The way that the rain can be falling on the back straight, where the track cuts through the Ardennes forest, while the start line is still bathed in sunshine? Or just the fact that the coffee's wonderful and Belgians are friendly and hospitable? I was jolted back into the real world by Pat Kearns. He slapped me on the shoulder, then settled himself into the chair opposite.

"What you doing buying your own food?"

"Dunno really, just saw it and–"

He cut straight across, to the point. "Heard any more about what happened to Mike?"

"Not a thing since the police pulled me in and–"

"According to Ray he was pulped. Can't figure out who the hell'd want to do that to him. You any ideas?"

I did have, but was still keeping them to myself. Pat'd never be able to keep it to himself. "No, not really. All a bit strange. Any news yet on when the funeral is going–"

"According to Ray, who's been talking to his Mum, the Coroner cleared the body for release this week and she's arranging it for the end of next week, probably Thursday afternoon."

"I ought to get his Mum's number off Ray. I'd like to go. He was allright, Mike. She's quite local isn't she?"

"Just outside Brackley I think. Presumably that's where the funeral'll be. Anyway, I'd better get back to the pits. I only came out here for some fags."

As Pat walked away, back towards the paddock gates, I wondered which drawer my black tie was in.

"Good morning. The usual?"

"Oh go on then..."

I smiled at Annie as I sat down at an empty table in GTD's hospitality unit. Even that early – it wasn't even eight – there were already a dozen or so mechanics and engineers sitting around having breakfast. If things went well it would give them a good start to the day, if they went badly once the cars were out on the track it might be the last thing they manage to eat in daylight. I said hello in response to greeting from a couple of the lads, pulled my book out of the bag dropped on the floor alongside my chair, and started reading. I hadn't got beyond the first paragraph of the chapter detailing Senna's time spent living in the spare bedroom of a photographer in Bramhall when Ray Otley appeared alongside me and sat down. As he sat he nodded a private code message to Annie. Minutes later we both got breakfast platters at the same time. He started to talk.

"Pat said you're planning to go to Mike's funeral. I spoke to his mother yesterday morning and it's at her local church then the crematorium in Brackley. Eleven next Thursday. Do you want to ring her or should I let her know?"

"I'll ring her, but I could do with you letting me have her number–"

"No problem. I'll give it to you later. No, I'll ring her and let her know."

As we ate we talked about the mystery that still surrounded Mike's death. I learned that the police had told him Mike had been beaten up, and his death was due to a massive blow to the side of the head with that classic tool, the Blunt Instrument. An inquest had opened and adjourned so that the body could be released to his family, and the police were pretty clueless about the reason for the murder. I kept my own counsel about the Tel Martin connection. As the contents of our plates disappeared we moved the conversation on to more immediate and local matters.

"So how are the cars shaping up?"

"Good. We were fastest in unofficial practice yesterday, but everybody was trying out all sorts of different kit, so you can't really make anything of that session–"

"And what about the new cars?"

"All on schedule. Nothing radical – why mess with a good package and there are no major rule changes."

"Same drivers?"

"Yeah, got another two seasons with Will, he's a gem to work with. And Tim Whitely'll be with us for at least next season. He's after a raise but I told him that we'll discuss that when he starts out-performing his team-mate. The usual stuff–"

"So when do you start testing? Are you booked for Estoril in January?"

"Yeah. Should be ready with both cars for then. If not we'll take one and see how it goes. You be going out there?"

Before Ray left we arranged to meet up that night at his hotel for a full team dinner with his sponsors. I was gathered my things together to head off and take a nosy around the paddock when Annie came over, put two cups of coffee on the table, and sat don in the chair opposite me. Everybody else had evaporated and there were just the two of us under the canvas awning.

"Aren't you doing a book on Marsport?"

"Yes. How'd you know?"

"No secrets in racing. Anyway, thought you might be interested to know that Tel Martin has just sacked his caterers. This is their last season..."

Another bit of intelligence. I thanked Annie for the information and the breakfast, and walked off to find some racing cars to watch.

When the flag dropped at a little after four on Sunday afternoon I felt deflated. The race had been held in clear late summer weather with no rain anywhere on the circuit. With Will Fellows having already lifted the title none of the drivers seemed that hungry. Will qualified in the middle of the pack and stayed there right through the race. Tim Whitely suffered a rare engine failure. His power unit had exploded in spectacular style, trailing a rooster-tail of thick bluish-white smoke the length of the straight. That robbed him of a clean second place behind race winner Paul Williams. The Premier-Porsche team had seized the moment and taken the other places on the podium. The result made no impact on the championship standings, just gave consolation prizes to a team sitting in the middle of the points table. I rattled off a couple of shots of the champagne spraying antics of the three blokes on the podium, then wandered back into the paddock.

I arrived near the Marsport cluster of trucks just in time to dodge out of the way of a first aid crew rushing from the nearby medical centre. The team's head trucker – who I presumed to be Geoff – was lying on the concrete nearby the tailgate of a transporter, and it looked as though he'd had a toolbox, a damned big bright red chest of Snap-On drawers full of spanners and sockets, dropped on his foot. He was writhing in agony until the medic gave him a face mask, and a few lungsful of gas and air.

Nice one, Tel. What I saw made me think of friendly fire. Like those British soldiers who were sacrificed during the Gulf War when an American pilot mistook their Warrior armoured vehicle for an Iraqi tank and 'neutralised' the threat they represented. And Tel's orders had been to neutralise the regular truckie as a prelude to whatever was due to unfold later that evening in a truck stop not far from Ostend.

I watched while the paramedics put an inflatable splint around the driver's leg and slid a rigid stretcher underneath him. As they carried him across the paddock to the medical centre I slipped quietly away, back to the media car park.

6
Things go better with gas

I'd parked up the car in a corner of the truck stop outside Torhout, switched off the lights, and sat waiting. The advantage of the chaos that was surrounding the injured Geoff was that it had bought me a little time. I had slipped away from the track and headed back to the rendezvous point that I overheard Tel and the limping man arrange in Barcelona. Figuring that I had a good hour to spare I locked up the car and walked across to the café, returning to my lurking Rover a couple of minutes later with a pastry and a styrene cup of cappuccino. Within a little while the packaging joined a stack of old MacCups and empty food bags and sandwich wrappers littering the front passenger footwell.

The daylight was starting to fade and the floodlights had come on when an unmarked German-registered blue Vito van pulled in. It parked up in the middle of the main parking area, just as I was wondering whether to go and get another drink. I would probably have taken no notice of the van if the driver hadn't stepped out and walked across towards the café. Even from almost a hundred yards away I recognised him; the silent one from the tapas bar, the one wearing the leather coat. The way he dragged his left leg was a dead giveaway. Like I'd already done, he reappeared a few moments later carrying a cardboard tray holding a drinks cup and a food bag. He got back into the Vito and disappeared from view.

I had to wait another half hour before the whoosh and hiss of a set of air brakes alerted me to the arrival of a truck. A forty tonner, shark grey and red with a whole run of logos along its shiny side panels. It pulled up alongside the Mercedes Vito, and its driver got down, walked around the front of the tractor unit, nodded to the man in the van, and carried on walking until he was halfway down the length of his trailer. He turned a key, opened up one of the stowage panels just above ground level, and started to pull out a couple of gas cylinders, one at a time.

About four feet long and maybe five inches in diameter, every race team has dozens of these bottles. Some are full of compressed air for running tools, others have oxygen and acetylene for welding. The pair that I watched being pulled out of their carrying rack looked light, so they were probably empty. It looked like Paul Stevenson moving them, but I couldn't be sure because despite the warm temperatures he was wearing a grey and red team jacket and matching baseball cap.

He carried them one at a time the few feet from his truck, returning with two more cylinders that had been handed to him by the limping man. I heard the side door of the Vito slide shut, then watched the driver come back around and get into his seat. The sound of his door slamming shut reverberated across the quiet truck stop. The blue van was already leaving the service area while I watched Stevenson locking his trailer compartment. A moment later the truck engine bust into life and it too pulled out of the parking lot and back onto the N33.

I had watched all the gas bottle activity in close up, through the telephoto lens which I aimed through the gap created by partly lowering the passenger door window of my car. I'd loaded the camera with ultra high speed film, but even so was unsure how good or not the photographs were likely to be; despite its floodlighting the truck stop's parking area seemed dark and gloomy. I'd worry about that later, though. I scooped up the rubbish from the footwell, got out of the car, stuffed the empty drink cups and paper bags into a wastebin, and then got myself back in, and on the road towards my return ferry.

Janice sat across from me in the booth. We were waiting for our main courses to arrive and were already threequarters of the way through our first bottle of Barolo.

"So how'd you get into... erm... erotic dancing? Known you all this time and you've never said, never really explained..."

"You mean stripping'? S'what it is really."

"Um."

"You ever noticed them posters in the sitting room at my place? The Covent Garden ones? I always wanted to be a ballet dancer and me Mum let me start taking lessons when I was eight. I used to go on the bus every Saturday morning to a place in South Norwood. Loved it. Even auditioned for the Royal Ballet when I was twelve. Didn't get in though."

"Why not?"

"Too tall. Even then–"

"But you aren't that tall. What are you? Five eight?"

"Well spotted. But all the Corps de Ballet are midgets, or at least they are when you're alongside 'em. I was like six inches taller, even then."

"So did you carry on with dancing lessons? Seems a bit unfair to have–"

"I was gutted, Bleedin' gutted. But I loved dancing anyway so I did some tap lessons..."

"But you kept falling in the sink?"

"Ha bloody ha. Anyway, I carried on 'til I left school. Went working for Woolworth's in Croydon. Bloody hated it. Then a mate of mine said that she's heard about auditions for go-go dancers up west. Job turned out to be in Dubai, a six month contract."

"So you went?"

"Yeah, brilliant time. Worked five nights a week, and had all day to sunbathe. Good money too. Got me the deposit together for the house. But towards the end it got a bit uncomfortable. So Elaine and me came back."

"Uncomfortable?"

"Yeah, some of the blokes were oil workers and they thought that 'cos we were dancing topless and they were paying for drinks they'd got the right to a feel."

She flicked her long nearly-natural blonde hair out of her eyes and sat back as the waiter arrived with our food. As she picked at her chicken fillet she started to talk again.

"So anyway, then I went and worked in an insurance office for a bit. Bleedin' hated it. Elaine moved up to town and started work at a club off Frith Street, stripping. She was earning good money and there was no hassle because there's lots of security around. So I gave it a shot too."

"Do you still work any clubs?"

"Not any more. More money in private parties. I'm nearly twenty eight. One day my arse'll start to spread and my tits'll have dropped, and I don't fancy plastic ones. It won't last forever so I'm getting it while I can. Wouldn't mind paying off the mortgage, and getting a little shop selling dancewear or something. But don't worry sweetheart, I've got a few years in me yet..."

"I'd have thought private parties and stag nights could get a bit dangerous..."

"Not really, our agent always makes sure that he sends a minder along. Just in case anything gets lairy."

"So I'd better not upset you then, in case you set your gorilla on me..."

"Bloody right Mark. Watch it!"

I left early the next morning and headed for home, and a cremation.

7

Spooks in the night

A vicar had been parachuted in to deliver the usual scripted platitudes. Telling us how good a guy Mike had been and how he would be missed by his small but close family – just a mother and a sister, so far as I could work out. And then he did the expected, warning us off doing strange things in back alleys because of the fear of thunderbolts and shit-trains from on high.

Despite Mike having such a small family, the chapel was full. Most of the GTD crowd turned up, as did a couple of lads I recognised from his local in Banbury. Granville and a uniformed policeman were there, too, sloping around at the back of the chapel. Then they watched everybody leave from a safe distance at the far side of the car park. They appeared at the crematorium, too, checking everybody out.

When I emerged Mike's mother was standing outside the crematorium, alongside the half dozen wreaths. She looked as though she wanted to read their dedication cards, but wasn't sure where to begin. A small lady who looked to be in her mid-sixties, she was wearing an unseasonably heavy black woollen coat and hat. Ray, stood just beyond her, saw me approach and moved to her side. Gently taking hold of her left elbow, he introduced me to her.

"Oh yes, Michael used to talk about you. Said you were always very good to him. Will you come back to the house? It isn't much but I'd be very pleased to have you come back. Mister Otley's coming back, aren't you..."

"Of course. And you'll be pleased to join us, won't you Mark?"

I stood by the rose bushes, enjoying the warmth of the sun against my back in the compact, neat garden of the compact, neat council house on the outskirts of Banbury. An empty teacup and saucer was in my left hand. I was looking around for somewhere to get rid of the burned-out cigarette that was in the other, when Mrs Lewis came out to me. I discreetly dropped the filter tip into the middle of a rose bush. She had shed the coat and hat and was wearing a lighter-weight simple black skirt and white blouse. When I looked into her face I could tell I had been mistaken about her age; she was no more than middle fifties. Losing her son had put a few years on her. Like it would.

"I'm terribly sorry…" I started to say.

"You were with him the night before he–"

"That's right. We'd been at Silverstone at the Jordan party, and I dropped him off." God, how to deal with this? I was probably the last friendly face he'd seen.

"Yes, Mister Granville told me. They've still no idea what… why…"

I was saved by a couple who appeared, interrupting us to tell her that they would have to get going. She excused herself, and went to see them off.

As I drove away from the estate an hour or so later I wasn't able to shake out of my head the image of Mike lying with a smashed face in the back alley. It phased in and out with the look of anguish worn by a mother who would never be able understand why her only son was murdered. And the arrogant smile that is usually on the face of Tel Martin.

"You off 'til next year, then mate?"

"I wish. No, the last round's coming up next weekend in France, I've a lot of other stuff to do, a book to get on with and I might get away towards the end of the year for a break but–"

"Still. I wouldn't mind a job like yours. Better than delivering parts to garages."

"It's a bit like sex, my job; fun for amateurs. But yes, it does beat working for a living."

We stood in the bar of the Marquis of Granby, me, Steve and Mikey. They are a couple of the regulars, guys much my own age, not mates exactly, but good people to drink with. We'd got to know each other because it is better than drinking alone.

The bar was quiet – it often is in the early evening in early autumn, once the tourists have buggered off – and, responding to Mikey's request, Frank the landlord pulled us another round of pints from the tapped and spiled barrels resting on a trestle behind the bar. "Aye, I'll have half with you. Cheers." As soon as he'd placed the full glasses in front of us he disappeared through the doorway at the back of the bar.

Apart from us there were only three other people in the bar; a couple sat across the room near the massive fireplace and a bloke sitting on his own in the corner, nursing a half of bitter and reading the Guardian. The bloke had come in five minutes after me; the couple were already there when I'd arrived.

I ambled out of the pub an hour or so later and started to walk back in the light of a nearly full moon, along the lane to the farm and an early night. I took the usual precaution of walking along the right hand side of the tree-lined lane, so that I could step onto the verge and out of the way in the unlikely event of anything coming down towards me. I was mildly surprised when a dark-coloured Omega came along behind me and slowed to a crawl.

"Mr McDermott?"

I was more than a touch cautious. "Who wants to know?"

The driver pushed the button and turned on the interior light, illuminating one side of his face. He flicked open a small wallet, showing an identity card. "My name's Sutherland. Customs and Excise. Would you mind getting into the car? Please?"

"What the... Why? What's it all about?"

"We need to talk."

I could think of no reason to avoid getting into the car, and walked around the back of it. As I closed the front passenger door I looked across at the driver.

"You were in the pub, weren't you?"

"That's right. But I though speaking to you there might be a little indiscreet. Do you mind if we speak at your home? It's just along the lane here, isn't it?"

Three minutes later we were sitting in the caravan. I pondered this weird twist of events. I had a feeling my plans for an early night were about to be wrecked by this visitor from the Customs. I offered him a drink, wondering how he'd connected me with what's been going on.

"Sorry about all the cloak and dagger stuff. You were seen by our colleagues in Belgium at a service area near Torhout. Would you mind telling me what you were doing there?"

I thought fast. "I stopped for a coffee."

"Isn't that a little strange, Mr McDermott? You stop for a coffee in a service area near Ostend, then drive off and get a ferry twenty kilometres up the road in Zebrugge? Why the detour?"

Paranoia. I knew what I'd been doing there, but suddenly had the feeling that I'd better play it straight or I could end up on the list of suspects. And about the last thing I needed was to be on the wrong side of the fence from a set of government spooks. "I was watching what I thought was a drug deal."

"Carry on."

"A couple of months ago I was tipped off that there was something weird going on in the racing scene. That someone in a team was using the industry as cover for moving drugs. And it led me to that truckstop." I then went on to explain all, the way that Mike had told me about his hunch and ended up dead. The conversation I had overheard in the tapas bar. The accident that had injured Geoff the truck driver.

"And you were taking photographs, weren't you?"

"Yes, but they're not processed yet. I've been busy, haven't got round to it."

"If you'd be good enough to let me have the roll I'll have our people–"

"No way. Sorry, but you can forget that. If you take the roll I'll never see them again, but if you like I can get you a set run off. I'll let you have them by the end of the week."

"We would rather have the–"

"No chance. They're mine and I'd like to keep it that–" I knew I was taking a punt on long odds, but wasn't prepared to lose control of something that might have some value.

"If you insist. But please let us have a set of them. Yesterday if possible."

He handed me a business card, and left. I watched through the window as he started his car, carried on watching until his tail lights disappeared down the narrow lane back towards the motorway. And wondered if there's a cupboard somewhere stuffed full of blokes like him, anonymous, ordinary, nondescript... Drag a new one out every time they need to build up the ranks.

I settled back onto the bench, studying the cream card. The portcullis crest, HM Customs and Excise Investigations Department, an address in South East One and a phone number. I scribbled his name on the back of it. The guy hadn't looked particularly threatening; not so much as a hint of being mad, bad or dangerous. But the detail they already had on me, that was something else... Where I live. Where I drink. What I'd been doing in a car park in Belgium.

Fuck.

It made sense to get a few more shots of Paul Stevenson at Magny-Cours. This was easy; I just rattled a few frames off as I wandered around the pitlane in the build-up to the first qualifying session. As I was putting the finished roll into my bag and fishing out a fresh film to load, my knuckles brushed against the pack of prints from Belgium. I'd decided to take them with me rather than stick them away in the safe back home. Instinct told me they'd be more secure with me.

I'd flown in from East Midlands straight to the circuit with Arcam Racing, the result of a need to talk to Vivien Reed for a feature I'd been asked to write. A quick hint to the team's press officer, complete with comparison of diaries, had been all it took. Not only to get me on their chartered 146, but also into the chateau they were all staying at, just down the road from the track. All at their expense. Neat.

"You going away after this?" Andy settled himself down alongside me.

"No. Got a book to write, and a few other bits and pieces to wrap up. Might get away over Christmas though..."

"How's your wife about all this zipping around you do?"

"I'm not married. Always managed to avoid it–"

"Wish I had. Mine's always going on to me to get a regular job back at the workshop. But then as soon as the season's finished and I've been around home for a month she complains that I'm under her feet... Kids complain too."

I'd been sitting quietly, drinking a styro cup of coffee on the blue-painted steel steps outside the press office, when I'd been joined by Andy, Vivien's chief mechanic. He took a cigarette out of a pack which he replaced in his shirt pocket, and fished in the pocket his shorts for a lighter. He lit the Gauloise and momentarily disappeared behind a cloud of thick blue smoke.

"I heard you're writing a book on the lover-ly Tel."

"At this rate there'll be no need for my publishers to do any advance publicity on the book. It seems everyone and his granny already knows about–"

"Yeah, well... Anyway, don't you reckon it's a bit odd he ain't here?"

"Isn't he?"

"No, and from what I've seen everybody's wondering why not, too. Don't forget that his lot's in the next pit to us. You should've heard Stevo goin' on earlier. Couldn't raise him at home, wasn't answerin' his mobile..."

Andy was distracted by a waving figure in the distance, someone dressed in an identical red and blue shirt to the one Andy was wearing. He stood, waved back then started to walk away. "See you later. My dinner's ready."

I drained my cup and despatched it into a bin by the bottom of the steps. Then lit another cigarette and sat down again to think. So where was Tel Martin? It was, as Steve said, a bit odd that he hadn't shown up for the last round of the season. I hadn't seen anything of him or spoken with him since Spa, but there was nothing unusual about that; things had been left that I would get together with him after this race. Or maybe he'd just breeze in later, as though that's what he'd had planned all along.

But he didn't show. When I asked Paul Stevenson about Tel's absence later in the afternoon I was told that it was a mystery to him, too. And he gave the impression of telling the truth.

8

A shrinking willie

The only substantial racing incident of the weekend was during qualifying. The cars are set up with the bare minimum, the lightest weight, of fuel. And the engine speed limiters are raised to give an extra few hundred revs; any advantage that can be squeezed out of the machinery offers the chance of being further towards the front of the grid. And even in a long distance race, a good grid position is important.

Premier-Porsche's race engineers had already pushed the boundaries as far as they dared, but Mick Rafferty seemed to think he could go just one degree further. Renowned for his on-the-edge style, Mick found the boundary of the handling envelope a couple of laps into his session, then burst through it a lap later when he turned left at the end of the Chateau d'Eau straight, then hard right into the Lycée corner, the last bend of the lap.

I watched this scenario unfold from where I stood trackside, behind a low concrete wall and ahead of a deserted grandstand. I was lining up to get a few shots through a monster telephoto lens when he came into my viewfinder. I could tell it wasn't right even before he committed to the final hundred and twenty degree curve, so I tracked through. The motor drive whirred through a freshly-loaded film as I followed the action. He clipped the outside edge of the rumble strips, put his left wheels onto the grass, and slid across into the barrier with a sickening thud. Slivers of bodywork flew through the dust, and there was a flash of flame that burned bright for a moment before the car's on-board extinguisher dealt with it. An eerie silence followed, cancelled out almost instantly by the roar of a marshall's 4x4 truck tearing out of its parking place a hundred yards down the track, towards the crumpled wreckage.

Mick Rafferty walked away from the shunt, and I walked back across the closed track towards the pits. I felt good, knowing that I'd just bagged some superb shots that I would be able to sell several times over. Mick would have less of a good feeling. He'd have a headache from the shunt and earache from his team, whose plans of a relaxed night at their hotel would have gone down the pan. They would be spending the night preparing the spare car for the race.

Tel Martin turned up at about eleven on Sunday morning. I was standing alongside the paddock fence talking to Sanjit, Arcam's press officer, alongside the rented people carrier we'd just arrived in from the Chateau. We watched the familiar shiny grey chopper drop into the helipad a quarter of a mile away. We saw Tel get straight out of the Jet Ranger, duck to counter the wind from the rotor blades and walk across the field, carrying just a small piece of baggage. He held his hand over his eyes to guard them from the dust being kicked up by the idling rotors. We carried on watching as he shook the briefcase and showed something to the customs officer who emerged from his shed by the gate. Tel carried on without stopping, and got onto the back of a waiting scooter driven by one of the Marsport team.

"Sorry Sanjit, better get back to the pits and do some work, need to justify the trip..."

"Allright man, see you later, yeah? Back here at five?"

Even though I had been in and out of the paddock a half dozen times during the previous twenty four hours, I still had to show the geek on the gate my laminate before he would let me through the full-height turnstile. I walked straight across towards the back of the Marsport trucks, but changed my mind. Instead of letting myself in through the back door of their pit garage I swerved at the last moment and went into Arcam's open door instead.

I smiled at a couple of the Arcam crew as I passed by, and carried on through the open front shutter. I settled myself on the top tier of the wooden bench at the front of the pit, against the wall between the two garages.

"So, where are we?" Tel's voice was clear.

"Sixth and eighth, guv–"

"Why does it always go fucking pear-shaped when–"

I could hear the pair of voices, Martin's and Stevenson's, without seeing either man. They were so close that I could tell they were just inside the frame of the open roller door to my right. I sat listening, camera in hand, messing with the aperture ring as though I was doing something important. Being deep into the smuggling operation was apparently not enough to save Paul Stevenson from a bollocking of royal proportions. Any privilege he had off the track evaporated when there was a race to be run.

"So what have you done?"

"Dialled in a bit more oversteer on Paul's car. But both are down on–"

"I don't pay you for excuses, I pay you for results."

He was a less-than-happy bunny. Maybe that sports psychologist was right; losing made Tel's Willie shrink.

As it worked out, Paul Williams did one of his conjuring tricks. He somehow managed to pull a win out of thin air, giving Marsport a last-gasp victory in the four hour race that wrapped up the season. I bumped into Tel Martin near Arcam's rented Espace when he walked past, heading for his waiting helicopter. He still had his briefcase in one hand, but in the other was a tasteless three foot high trophy. Its cheap gold plating and glass 'jewellery' caught the rays of the afternoon sun.

"Another one for the mantelpiece, eh Tel?"

He didn't say anything, just smirked and carried on past me, walking towards the little airfield.

"You'd better tell us what's been going on."

Nearly midnight on Sunday, three of us around the oak table in Hilda and Alf's kitchen. I'd just got back from the airport.

"What do you mean? Nothing... I mean..."

"Tell him what happened last night, Alf."

"What do you mean, last night? I wasn't here–"

But somebody was, weren't they Alf?"

As I sat drinking my second cup of tea from the pot that Hilda had brewed, I pondered over what Alf told me. How he'd heard the dog bark and the chickens start cackling, how he'd come out into the yard to see a couple of 'heavy looking blokes' trying to force the door of my caravan, and how, after shouting at them, did what he said any farmer would. He'd taken a pot-shot at them from a hundred yards away with his twelve-bore.

"You what?"

"I wasn't letting anyone just wander around–"

"But you're leaving yourself wide open to–"

"Bugger that. Anyway, I didn't hit 'em. Aimed wide. But I think I winged their car–"

"What was it? What were they driving?"

"Range Rover. Black'n, or dark grey or navy. Hard to tell at night."

"Anyway, what's it all about?" True to form, Hilda couldn't leave Alf to talk for longer than thirty seconds. "Two blokes trying to break into your place. You had that bloke around a couple of weeks ago, then there was that phone call from the police last month..."

I told them the bare minimum, that I was looking into something strange going on in the racing world, and that I'd given a lift to a bloke who a couple of days later had ended up on a stainless steel table at the Radcliffe. I was totally honest in telling them that I hadn't a clue who the two blokes in the Land Rover were, but that I'd ask the police if he was anything to do with them. I knew that if they'd been police they'd have already been around, complaining about being shot at, but there was no point saying that to Hilda and Alf. I wasn't comfortable lying to them, but something was telling me the less they knew, the safer they'd be.

I slept badly that night.

Sutherland sat opposite me in the caravan. I'd rung him Monday morning, telling him that I'd got his photographs. Before he turned up I'd taken the precaution of putting the negatives and the other set in the safe, out of sight under the very bench we were both sitting on.

"These are very good. Very useful."

"Thanks. I wasn't sure they'd be of any use, there wasn't much light around... Did any of your people pay me a visit on Saturday night?"

"Ours? No. Could be the police, possibly, but I doubt it. Not on a Saturday night... Why? What happened on Saturday anyway?"

I explained the events to him, leaving out the bit about Alf shooting at them. No point saying anything about that unless I have to. He sat silently while I talked. He repeated that the visitors were nothing to do with him.

"Thought not. I'm going to ring DI Granville anyway, but like you I'm not sure–"

"I'll speak to Granville. So what did they look like?"

I outlined that they hadn't been close enough for Alf to describe them, other than they looked big and were dressed in dark clothes. I decided against telling him that they'd been on the receiving end of an Eley No7 cartridge, figuring that if they were legitimate then they'd have already been back.

He didn't ask for the negatives.

I left the farm a couple of minutes after him, and headed to the hardware store in Wheatley to invest in an extra lock for the caravan door. They might not try again, but then they just might.

Tel's muscle? Mike's murderers? Maybe.

I had just finished screwing the cover plate of the new mortise lock into place when my phone rang.

"Sutherland. I checked with Inspector Granville and as I thought, none of his people have been anywhere near your home. He wanted to know why anybody should have been taking a look at you, and was interested in talking to you himself but I suggested that he can leave it to us–"

"Very good of you."

"Um. Anyway, I don't suppose your cousin – is he your cousin? – Managed to see anything of the index plate of the vehicle, did he?"

"No. Like I said, it was a bit far off and it was past midnight."

"And you've no idea of who it might have been? Have you anything on our friend that would make him suspicious?"

I explained again to Sutherland that I wasn't in possession of anything particularly incriminating. Nothing that anybody beyond him or me knew about, anyway. Eventually, he'd rung off.

I had no sooner pulled the ring on a can of Stella and flicked on the television to check the early evening news when a shiny-new dark blue Vauxhall pulled into the yard and parked up alongside my Rover. Bloody Granville.

"Sorry to trouble you Mr McDermott, but..."

There's always a but. A but that means more bloody hassle.

"... I am given to understand from my colleague at HM Customs and Excise..."

Dear God, save me from an idiot who insists on talking like he's reading out a statement in front of a magistrate.

"...That you have a theory about the death of Mr Lewis. Would you mind explaining it to me?"

Oh sure. He sat looking at me from the same seat that His Colleague from HM Customs and Excise had been in earlier. I attempted to distract him.

"Beer? Tea? Coffee?"

"Not for me thanks. Just an answer."

Bugger. So I told him as much as I had already told Sutherland. No more and no less.

"So why didn't you tell me this when you were at the station?"

"I wasn't sure about it then. It only started falling into place later."

"And how realistic do you think it is that this Martin will be involved? It strikes me as him having a little too much to lose–"

"There's a lot at stake."

"That's as may be. So where can I find him?"

"If you go blundering in – forgive my cynicism – you'll probably not achieve anything. And anyway–"

"I have already told Mr Sutherland that my involvement will be strictly arms-length. Do you have a photograph of Martin?"

"Only a transparency. Can you manage with that? I could get you a print off–"

"I'm sure our people could manage to do that. They are professionals you know–"

"Yeah. But remember, the most important thing is not to spook Martin. I know him and he's a slippery bastard. And ruthless with it..."

Granville eventually went away clutching the slide of Martin, and promising me that he'd tiptoe around the enquiry. Which presumably meant that they'd pull Tel out of his house at dawn and spend all day grilling him. Wonderful. I watched three minutes of some stupid game show, and decided to do the mature thing. I'd go down to the pub.

I pulled into the yard at Marsport at just before midday. Parking up in the spot labelled for visitors, I walked through towards the canopied main entrance of the silver-glazed three story building. Skirting around the back of a late-model navy blue XK-R with a personal plate that spelled out TCM, Terence Charles Martin.

Alongside Tel's Jaguar was another expensive sports car, a pale blue metallic Mercedes-Benz SL500. A German executive from Daimler-Benz once told me that they always sell that model in pairs; businessmen buy one for their mistress, and then get racked with guilt and order up another one for the wife. I wondered if Tel had bought one or two. I signed in at the desk, and was handed a Day Visitor pass. Then a young female arrived and led me up a flight of open stairs, knocked on a door and opened it immediately, standing aside to let me through. Tel came padding across the room and shook my hand, then turned and led me back to the desk he'd been sitting at.

"You met Lianne?"

Tel nodded towards the other desk, half a mile away over the expanse of rich blue Axminster that covered his office floor. A blonde was sat behind it. Her hair was piled up on top of her head. She wore a red silk suit that didn't look as though it had come from Top Shop, and forty kilos of gold; Bracelets, a sparkling ring that was probably worth more than my car, and a 1980s necklace. The kind with welded-together letters that usually state the name of the woman. Hers read 'bitch'. She looked a good three inches taller and ten years younger than Tel.

"Nice to meet you."

"You too. Terry has told me about you writing a book. Can't think who'd want to read it, though."

She'd stood and moved across the room to greet me, but instead of going back around the modern light oak desk and sitting back down, she leaned across and picked up her handbag. A long slender leg, wrapped in sheer silk stocking and finished by a four inch stiletto heel, stretched out as she gathered up the piece of rich red Prada luggage.

"See you again." She gave me a gleaming smile, a row of perfectly white, perfectly shaped teeth. Then turned towards Tel, who stood in the middle of the floor. "I'm going to town. See you tonight, Hon..." With a wave of her fingers and a waft of Chanel she was gone.

"I didn't realise your wife was involved in the business–"

"Keeps her amused, and gives her an income of her own. Still does all her shopping on the company Amex, though."

Over the next couple of hours Tel and I talked, first in his office then in the steak house a mile away. I learned that he and Lianne had no children "Neither of us had particularly wanted any..." and that life for Tel was dominated by his racing activities; all around his office and right down the staircase into reception were prints of racing cars, many of them photographs of him at the wheel of a succession of 1970s machines. One wall of his office was lined with glass shelves, each one laden with glittering and garish trophies. Concealed lighting made sure that each statue, plaque and cup was shown to its best advantage.

He spoke of his father, who had encouraged him into starting racing by giving him an old car even before he was old enough to drive on the road. How he'd spent all his weekends and school holidays in the workshop at the dealership rebuilding and restoring his old Austin, learning what makes cars work and how to fix them.

He told me how his parents had both been killed when they were driving down to their place in Spain almost twenty years ago. A truck had pulled out of a side road on the far side of Gerona. His father's Jaguar was virtually on the junction, too fast and too close to take avoiding action. They'd run straight into the side of the truck and both died instantly. And how he and Lianne and his sister had been left everything.

"If it hadn't been for the old man, I'd have never got this..." he declared as we walked back into reception after lunch. "He taught me the ropes, taught me about the industry, taught me everything I know."

Then he showed me around the facility, allowing me to put my head through the doorway of the design room, where a half-dozen men and a single woman were beavering away at computer terminals. I was aware that all I could see were people at work, not the details of the work they were doing.

He showed me the workshops where several part-finished chassis sat in clinical white-tiled surroundings. Every so often he went off and spoke to somebody or other out of my earshot. I was treated to a whistle-stop tour of the whole of Marsport's three acre site, the moulding shop, the stores, the whole place.

As we walked out of the back door of the loading bay, we skirted the tail of a brand new transporter, a forty-foot panelled trailer that looked as though it had just been sprayed metallic grey, a gleaming canvas ready to take fresh livery. I spotted a dark green, nearly black, Range Rover parked up against the fence. It looked abandoned, a long way from all the other cars and vans parked up outside the workshops. I tried to check it out as we carried on walking.

"Do you still have the dealership?"

"Yeah, but my sister's husband runs it for us. Why?"

"Just wondered..."

We were getting tantalisingly close to the Range Rover. But the side I could see, the driver's side, looked undamaged. It was filthy with mud and spray, but there was no sign of any holes from shotgun pellets. As I spoke I was desperately thinking of a way to look around its other side, but couldn't come up with anything. Eventually I gave up and we walked back towards my car.

"I could do with coming down again to–"

"What for? Haven't you got enough of my background?"

"Yes, it isn't that, it's that I could do with some pics of the facility..."

"Can you give me time to get the place tidied up? Oh, and we're off for a long weekend to the Canaries again on Friday, so leave it 'til next Tuesday or Wednesday, then give me a bell. "

"Course. Anyway, the light's already going for today."

We left it at that, I'd come back within a couple of weeks. I got back to my Rover and scribbled down the index plate of the Range Rover on a scrap of paper, then fired up the car. It occurred to me as a drove out of the gates that I was taking a shine to the charming bastard. What a pisser.

9
Who Dares, Fails

Whatever else Tel had planned, the chances were he'd be carrying it around in his head rather than having it written down anywhere. But as I drove back around the M25 it occurred to me that there might be some mileage in taking a look around his place at the weekend, whilst he and the lovely Lianne were topping up their tans in Tenerife, lounging in Lanzarote or wherever it was they were going to. I had nothing else planned...

Which is why on that Friday night I was dressed in a black tracksuit, trainers, gloves and black woolly hat, poking about in the substantial gardens of Chez Martin.

It had been pretty easy to find the house, and I'd taken the precaution of driving past it a couple of times then parking up in the entrance to a field a few hundred yards down the lane. Hopefully nobody from the handful of neighbouring houses would have even noticed my car, and it would be out of sight from anybody driving past.

I was shaking like a leaf as a walked back towards the house. Problem Number One was that the electric gates were closed, and the side gate was locked, too. So I went around the back and climbed over the wall at its farthest point from the lane, where it backed onto the woods. Fortunately its design was scalloped, and was only five feet or so high at its lowest point.

I dropped onto the garden side, silently onto grass that felt like a carpet. I couldn't see a damned thing. Total blackness. Remembering something from an SAS manual I'd read years ago, I stood stock still with my eyes closed tight and counted slowly to sixty. When I opened them again I could make out the silhouette of trees ahead of me, and see the mist of my breath in the cold night air. The contents of my stomach were doing somersaults; Who Dares Farts.

As my vision improved I could make out the shape of the house about forty yards away. I started to walk slowly towards the building. I'd got about halfway when I was blinded by a floodlight that suddenly came on. I froze for a second like a startled rabbit caught in the headlamps of an approaching truck, then decided that I might as well make a run for the house. As I pressed myself against the corner brickwork I tried to recall if there was anything in the SAS book about glaring floodlights, but couldn't remember.

It all went dark again after what seemed like an hour but was probably forty seconds. It was silent. I edged around the side of the house, and found the back door. It was locked. So I carried on around until I got to a set of patio doors, but they were locked too. Same for the front door. Like the kitchen door, it had a mortise lock, not a Yale that I could have got past by slipping a credit card down the edge of the door jamb. Looking though the letterbox I could see a small red light glowing on the wall opposite, decided it was an alarm system pilot, and concluded that I'd better give up. I slipped back to the corner, hugging the brickwork, then decided to make a run for the back wall. The floodlight flashed on again, throwing a long shadow ahead of me as I headed for the way out.

As the car started up I decided that any career plans of becoming a burglar should be abandoned. Writing is safer.

Even though the season was over and things should have been quiet, the next week disappeared into a haze of activity. The caravan got a blitz-clean. I knocked out a couple of filler items for magazines, spend a comfortable half day sitting around in the tiny bar of the Two Chairman off Trafalgar Square talking to Will Fellows about his days with Marsport and about life in general. And went to the ballet.

Going there was part of a trade-off I did with Janice. She agreed to come with me to the Touring Car Awards dinner on Saturday, a best frock occasion. But only if I'd go and watch the Kirov's production of Petrouska with her at the South Bank the night before.

"It wasn't anything like as boring as I'd expected."

"Good ballet isn't."

"And that was good ballet, then?"

She thumped my shoulder, then laughed a deep, dirty, throaty laugh as we headed into the bar of the Royal Vic on Waterloo Road, nearby where I'd parked the car.

We spent the day in between the ballet and the dinner ambling around Notting Hill and Bayswater, while she tried – and failed – to find some new shoes that she liked, shoes to go with the outfit she'd be wearing that night at the Hilton.

"What about this place?"

"Too cheap. They look really tacky."

"How about here..."

"I'll try that pair…"

"What do you reckon?"

"I reckon I'll wear the ones I brought with me. And I reckon you're not very good at being with someone shopping for shoes. Should we go in here for some lunch?"

The dinner was the usual thing, lots of fake surprise when awards were handed out, a couple of bread roll fights, and too much free red wine. And real surprise on my part when we were walking into the ballroom for a bop around, and we bumped into Tel and Lianne Martin. I introduced Janice to them. They both headed off to the cloakroom, and Tel and I walked across to the bar together. He asked what we were drinking, and as we waited for the barman I couldn't help asking him the obvious question.

"I didn't expect to see you here. Didn't realise you had anything to do with Touring Cars–"

"Invited by… Got invited. Might be moving into running a Touring Car team next season. Don't know yet."

"New team?"

"No, taking over one of the existing ones. But it's early days, haven't decided. So nothing in print, yes?"

"Of course. But you'll let me know–"

We were interrupted by the barman putting the drinks on the bar. Then Janice and Lianne reappeared. We found a table, and the four of us sat down together. The band played while we all made small talk. Janice heard the band burst into a medley of Abba stuff and dragged me, unwillingly, out of my seat. She and I danced together for a few minutes, then my lack of dexterity overwhelmed her and she conceded. We went back to the table. A few minutes later, when the quartet's sax player was massacring the intro to Gerry Rafferty's *Baker Street*, Lianne suddenly sprang up and grabbed my hand. "Dance with me. Terry never dances."

Where Janice had swooped and swirled around the floor ahead of me, Lianne took my hands and we settled into a sort of smooch-with-spaces. We abandoned the floor when the band burst into *Rock Around the Clock*. Shortly afterwards Tel drained his whisky and coke and they left.

"I reckon she fancies you."

"What?"

"That Lianne. I reckon you could have her if you played your cards right."

I was sat on the bed in our room, undressing, when Janice delivered this particular judgement through the doorway. Whatever conversation was left remained unsaid when she appeared from the bathroom, wearing nothing but a smile.

We checked out of the hotel on Sunday morning, me feeling pretty content with life. And grateful that Ford had picked up my bill. We didn't say much as I drove through the quiet backstreets of South London to drop Janice off at her place. It occurred to me as I headed home that this was the longest time we'd ever spent together. And it wasn't bad, either. All the same I was glad to get back to the comfort of my own company.

I was up early on Wednesday morning to take up the invitation of a computer company. They'd asked me to come along to Silverstone to show off their latest gizmos, the high-technology stuff that "helps winning cars keep on winning races" as their publicity bloke put it.

I chatted over coffee to a couple of their people, but declined the visit to the pits – I probably knew more about what went on there than the PR man did. Instead I went trackside, and watched a couple of the cars slip-sliding through the complex as they ran shakedown laps through the misty morning. A damp track and monster amounts of power tests the abilities of tyre manufacturers and skills of drivers – and is a damned sight more interesting to watch than some presentation about the way that nerds with laptops make things happen in the racing world.

As well as Triplc A Racing, the team the computer people were technology-partnering, there were also cars there from GTD and Arcam. So after nearly losing the will to live following a post-lunch presentation, I escaped for a few minutes and sought out Ray Otley.

Ray offered me a coffee from the flask sitting on a bench at the back of their pit garage. I declined, and he made some comment about needing to make a note of me turning down something free. I ignored him and asked if he knew any more about Mike.

"Not heard a thing. Police haven't been near since I can't remember when. His Mum rang me a couple of weeks ago – seems she hadn't heard anything from them either."

"It's been a couple of months. Do you reckon it's been shoved down the pile?"

"Wouldn't surprise me..."

We left it that we'd ring the other if either of us heard anything. After returning to the hospitality suite and thanking my hosts for the lunch I picked up their information pack and yet another free T shirt and baseball cap. Then I headed back to the car park.

I'd just started cleaning off the mist from the side glass of my mud-spattered Rover when I felt a presence. As I turned around the world went red when a punch landed in my stomach, followed almost instantly by another that got me foursquare on the nose, erupting it.

“Just fuckin’ leave it… back off.” The words phased and faded as my sight turned from red to black.

I came around in the medical centre, with a paramedic stood over me, checking my blood pressure on a monitor screen.

“Welcome back.”

“Urgh…”

“You look worse than you are…”

He moved in close, and shone a bright light into each eye. It hurt.

“There doesn’t seem to be any evidence of concussion. Your nose is broken, though. It’ll heal, there’s no point strapping it, just try not to blow it hard for a few days… If I was you I‘d get home and put my feet up for a day or two.”

My head still hurt.

“Who’ve you been upsetting, then?”

“Uuur…”

My head felt like lead, and there was blood all down the front of my shirt. It was Pat Kearns who was speaking to me. He moved closer as the medic moved away. I asked him if he knew what had happened.

“I’d wandered out into the paddock for a fag, and saw a car slip-sliding away out of the car park. Then I saw you lying by the side of your car. You were spark out, mate.”

“Uur, probably would still be–”

“Yeah, got the paras to come over and help. They stretchered you back here–”

“What was the car?”

“Couldn’t really tell, looked like a Land Rover though.’

“Range Rover?”

“Yeah, think it was. Someone you know after you?”

“Looking that way. Tell you later.”

“You want me to sort someone to drive you home? Won’t be a problem…”

“No, thanks Pat, but I’ll wait here for a bit and then–”

“Anyway, take it easy, mate. I better get back, They’ll be wondering where I got to…”

After a few more minutes and a glass of water two wash down the two pain killers I’d been handed in a little plastic cup, I persuaded the paramedics that I was allright, and that I’d be fine to drive. I eased myself back upright so my feet were on the ground, and discharged myself from their care. When I got back to the car it was starting to go dark. I wiped the side glass with a scraper, then sat with the motor running for a few minutes before I pulled off and headed for home. It took me what felt like several hours to cover the thirty minutes back to the farm.

I had no painkillers anywhere. I searched every cupboard and my camera bag to no avail, and didn't fancy going across the yard and having to explain to Hilda how I'd taken a pounding at the track. So I cracked open a bottle of brandy and drank my headache into sweet oblivion.

The following morning I had a pair of perfect cartoon-style black eyes. My nose was half its usual width again, and I couldn't breathe through it. And I had a monster hangover.

"Who've you been upsetting?"

This was the third time I'd been asked that question in two days. Hilda and Alf had wanted to know when I went over to pick up my post, so I told them that I reckoned it was something to do with the blokes at the farm. And the girl on the desk at the filling station in Wheatley was curious, too. Now I was having to explain, in considerably more detail, to Sutherland.

"Somebody jumped me at Silverstone on Wednesday. I was clearing the glass of the car. They punched my lights out and told me to back off."

"From what?"

I gave him a look that I hoped, through my distorted features, said 'what the fuck do you think?' We sat in a booth across from the bar of a pub in Uxbridge, a place picked because it would take us each as long to get there, me from home and him from his office in Southwark. It was the middle of Friday afternoon but was already going dark. It hadn't really got light all day. He took my expression on board and continued talking. "You're getting into this a bit too deep for comfort, obviously."

"Obviously."

"So what have you been doing to upset our man?"

I told him that I'd taken a quick look around his house, but that when I'd been with Martin earlier in the week he'd seemed fine.

"Could just be an act. Did he see you when you were looking around? And did you find anything?"

"I doubt it. They were in Lanzarote or somewhere..."

"So this was the weekend before last?"

I started to say "How did–" then stopped. Of course. Customs will have access to the details of anybody moving in or out of the country through regular channels.

"He has cameras around the house. Didn't you look for them?"

"Didn't occur to me."

"You're useless at undercover stuff."

This was accompanied by a wry smile, the first time I'd seen anything approaching humour in Sutherland's demeanour. Maybe he's human after all. And there was me, having him figured as an android.

I sat back and said nothing. This usually achieves the other person starting to talk. But Sutherland sat back too. He'd probably read the same guide to interview techniques. Eventually I gave up. "I'm not at all comfortable with this whole bloody scene. I'm out of my league. I'm a magazine hack, not an investigative reporter–"

"So it seems."

We eventually struck an agreement. I would share all of my information with them in return for them not giving me a hard time when the book is ready.

"You'll have to wait until we've secured a conviction, of course–"

"I'm committed to publishing next spring."

"We can sort that. I'm sure we can bring your publisher around to understanding our predicament. I'm sure the last thing they would want to do is get caught up in a prosecution for breaking the rules of sub judice... And you'll have to try and come to some similar arrangement with the police about the death of that chap, Mr... "

"Lewis. Mike Lewis."

"Yes, him. The last time I spoke to DI Granville they didn't seem to be any closer to finding anything positive. I asked them not to get too close to Martin, by the way... We can pull rank when we need to."

"But how close are you getting to Martin?"

"As close as our very limited resources will allow."

Which I took to mean that if it didn't pop up on a computer screen or drop into their laps, it didn't get checked out.

It turned out that I was wrong. Very wrong.

10

Back in the low life...

Although it was almost a week after the incident at Silverstone when I drove back across to Essex, I still looked like a panda.

"Jesus, who've you been upsetting?"

Tel seemed genuinely surprised when he shook my hand. Which surprised me.

"Don't know. Whoever it was blind-sided me." No point in making anything too obvious. No point in saying any more about it, either. I changed the subject. "Mind if I get a couple of shots of you outside the building, you know, the 'man and his empire' stuff?"

Tel disappeared up the stairs, which he took two at a time, and returned a moment later wearing a tie and a thousand poundsworth of Hugo Boss suede jacket. He looked every inch the millionaire race team owner that central casting would send in response to a request from a television director. As I rattled off the shots he played the part, too. This was a man in control. I'd have to play him at his own game.

Within an hour I'd got all the pictures I needed of the entire facility. Tel suggested lunch.

"How can I get hold of a few copies of your book? It'd be a good idea to give 'em out to our sponsors and a few other people. That's what Clive says, anyhow. Do I get a discount?"

Marsport's commercial manager might think again when he sees what's in the book.

"I'll get the publishers to let you know. I don't have anything to do with it once I've delivered the words and pictures to them–"

"So is there much money in writing books, then?"

The lunch went smoothly. Even though the holiday was still six weeks off, the steak house had a couple of Christmas parties in full swing. Tel and I sat in a distant corner, away from the noise of whoopee whistles, shrieks of piercing laughter and ever-louder chatter. We talked about the racing scene in general, about people we'd both known over the years, and about the mechanics and logistics of the publishing world. Of the difference in writing articles and writing books. He seemed genuinely interested.

Driving home later I had to consciously remind myself that this was a soon-to-be-convicted drug dealer, and that starting to actually get on with the bloke wasn't a smart idea. I brought back into my mind the image of Mike Lewis lying dead in an alleyway, and regained a sense of perspective.

The next four days were spent making a start at writing the book. I spent solid days at my computer putting the basic framework into place, the early story of Tel's life gleaned from the discs filled during my interviews and from the mountain of copies of features. I worked feverishly, starting early and finishing late, and by Saturday night I'd got to the point of starting to deal with the present. I glanced at the clock, realised it was almost eight, and started backing up my work ready to put it in the safe. I was deciding whether to order a take-away, or go out for an Indian, when my mobile rang.

"Sutherland. They've done another bottle swap."

"When? There's no racing going on."

"Our Belgian friends picked up on your chap Stevenson–"

"You make it sound like he works for me–"

"You know what I mean. Stevenson was flagged by the system coming off a ferry at Zebrugge yesterday morning. He was in a van, one of the team's. He drove to a factory just over the border into Holland, and picked up some packages."

"And was that what he had the–"

"No. They were quite legitimate, Brake components, apparently. He went back towards the ferry–"

"Don't tell me. He went into the truck stop…"

"Right. He met up with the same chap again, swapped two gas bottles over, and carried on back. This time they were good enough to let us know as things were actually happening, rather than several days later…"

"And you followed him off the ferry–"

"What do you think?"

"Erm, forgive my cynicism, but why are you telling me all this?"

Sutherland said that he'd promised to help me if I helped them, and continued by saying that the van was still under surveillance; it was parked up in a disused warehouse, and Stevenson had left it. Then he told me the real reason for the call.

"We would appreciate a little help from you in identifying some people."

"Can I bring a camera?"

"Don't be facetious, Mark..."

This was the first time he'd ever referred to me by name. I took it as a sign that he must be genuine about needing my help. I agreed to meet him in the pub in Uxbridge in an hour. For food I made do with a chocolate bar picked up when I fuelled the car.

We sat in his car in the car park, looking at a sheaf of grainy photographs.

"This is the man with the limp. He's a Dutchman named Piet van Drel. Interpol have him in the frame for a raft of 'problems' but so far they haven't been able to get him on anything. They're hoping that this time they'll have him, but we need proof that he's actually moving cocaine or heroin..."

"Don't these show him–"

"All they show is him moving gas cylinders. And although there's doubtless some minor charge attached to moving medical supplies without a gas bottle–"

"Take your point."

"And I take it this is Stevenson?"

"Yeah, that's him."

"Who are these other two though? Any ideas?"

He spread a set of pics across his lap, and passed them to me one at a time. I looked closely at them, but all I could make out were a couple of stockily-built men, middle forties, possibly older, white, dressed in dark clothes.

"Sorry, don't recognise either of them. Could be anybody. Are these the only pics you have of them?"

"We came across them talking to Stevenson in a pub in Kensal Green last week. Any idea why he should be there, by the way?"

"It isn't a place that's renowned for its racing components... Can I have a couple of shots of these guys, in case I come across them anywhere?"

Surprisingly, he handed me a colour print of the two together. It might come in useful when I get toward the end of the Martin book. Wonder if they drive a Range Rover? I Remembered that I'd never given Sutherland the registration number of the one I'd seen parked up Martin's compound. I fished it out from my pocketbook and handed it to him. "Sorry its incomplete, but if you can find out whose it is–"

"We should be able to get that checked."

11

Christmas presence

On a whim, and desperate to get away from the cold, grey damp of early December, I booked a week away in Lanzarote. I asked Alf to keep an eye on things at the caravan, persuaded Hilda to drive me to Gatwick, and went within twenty four hours of seeing the card in the Oxford travel agent's window.

Travelling on my own has never been a problem; the only down-side to being alone in strange places is that I can tend to think too much. The cure for that was to go for long walks along the promenades of Puerto del Carmen, stopping regularly at bars. Have a drink, do some people watching, read for a little while, then stroll on again. I spent one day on a bus tour around the island, Not the sort of thing I would ever think of doing, but easier that resisting the hard sell of a courier in the hotel reception. Apart from being the youngest person on the bus by at least one generation it wasn't that bad. I particularly enjoyed the stop-off at a vineyard in the middle of the island. I bought a tacky corkscrew with a handle made from a polished piece of twisted vine trunk, as a thank you for Hilda. Then decided that I'd better get her something to open, so bought a couple of bottles of the local white wine.

I arrived home two weeks before Christmas feeling recharged from a week of warm sun, plenty to eat and drink, and lazy mornings on a balcony reading four airport novels in a row. I was relieved to hear from Hilda, as she drove me home from the airport, that there'd been no visitors. Unwelcome or otherwise.

There were fourteen messages waiting on my voicemail when I switched my mobile back on as Hilda bullied her way through traffic on the M25. Not many people are brave enough to take on a battered Land Rover with bull bars front and rear.

Three of the messages were from Sutherland, and all but one other were work-related. I could deal with all of them later. It was the other one that intrigued me, but first I needed to check up with Sutherland. I waited until I was in the caravan, huddled alongside the heater.

He knew that I'd been abroad for a break, but was pissed off that I hadn't let him know I was going.

"I booked it at the last minute. Anyway, since when do I have to report to you?"

"You're quiet right. But something has come up. Martin hasn't been seen for more than a week."

"Eh? He's not just gone away? They've got a place in the Canaries, I think–"

"If he has, he didn't fly out of a British airport."

He ought to have been able to tell I'd been to Lanzarote, too. Or maybe he did, and just wasn't letting on.

"What about his wife? Is she around?"

"She is."

We left it that I'd ring around a few of my contacts, to see if anyone had spotted Tel in the last few days. I made the calls, but nobody had. The other intriguing call might bring an answer more quickly anyway – it was from Lianne Martin. I called the mobile number she'd left at the end of her message.

"Hi Lianne, it's Mark McDermott. Returning your call."

"Who? Oh, Mark... Thanks for getting back to me. What are you doing on Sunday afternoon?"

"Nothing planned, just got back from a week away and I've a few things to sort out, but nothing on Sunday. Why?"

"We're having a few drinks at home. Can you make it? It'd be good to see you–"

"Be delighted."

Not to mention fascinated. She gave me the address and some cursory directions, telling me to watch out for the high brick wall just past the cross-roads, and was gone. I rang Sutherland again – making a mental note to ask him his first name – and told him.

"And did she say 'we'?"

"Yes. We."

"You will let me know who's there, won't you?"

I assured him that I would, and also found out that his christian name was Nigel. It would be.

Friday found me in an Oxford wine bar, at the Christmas party for Diamond Life Racing. I'd received the invite a couple of weeks before heading off on holiday, and stood having a drink with a couple of the engineers when we were interrupted.

"Mark mate. Got any rubber gloves on you?"

"What?"

"Rubber gloves. You know, Marigolds..." Chris, one of the service van drivers, was interrupted by a thump on his shoulder. But he carried on. "S'Dave here. Got the full works a couple of weeks back..."

I turned towards Dave, the team's engine builder who was stood alongside Chris with an inane grin on his not-altogether-sober face.

"He was on way back from the 'Ring when customs stopped him–"

"And gave me the third degree..." interrupted Dave. "Dunno what it was all about. Pulled me into a shed, took the entire bleedin' rig apart. Van, trailer, race car, whole bleedin' lot. Last nut and bolt."

"What were you doing at Nürburgring? Isn't on your usual–"

"Took my own car. remember, I picked up that ex-works Escort Turbo last year? Always wanted to give it a proper run, and always fancied a run round the full circuit at the 'Ring. Just for the hell of it. Weather was looking promising, so I took a week off and went over there, trailing it behind my camper..."

He then went into explicit detail about how he'd been given the full body search as well, and kept for a couple of hours before being let go on his way back home. I thought it was just one of those fun things that I came across now and then. Only when I was in the cab on my way back home did I make the connection. That Dave's surname was Martin.

I made an effort for Sunday, pulling out and pressing up my one good suit, wearing it with a newly-bought shirt and a bright tie that I'd picked up in the services at Cherwell Valley. I got to the house at about half past three in the afternoon. This time, instead of hiding my car in the entrance to a field down the road, I swept straight through the open gates and parked up alongside a red Ferrari Testarossa. As I walked across towards the front door I glanced up and saw a bracket on the corner of the house, just below the gutter line. It held a pair of matching security cameras, facing in opposite directions.

"Mark, so glad you could make it! Are you alone?"

Lianne answered the door to me dressed in a slinky black dress with an impressively low-cut top that revealed a substantial cleavage. I tore my eyes away from her breasts and up to here face, and thanked her for inviting me, asking if it was allright that I was on my own.

"Of course, no problem at all. Let me get you a drink–"

She was interrupted by the doorbell ringing again, so she turned and started back down the hallway, telling me she'd catch up with me in a few minutes. I followed her pointed directions towards the lounge where, she'd said, I would find a drink. A dozen couples were standing around, several of whom nodded a guarded hello as I picked up a glass of wine. The only familiar faces were Paul Stevenson and Clive Allen, both with women I took to be their wives.

We said hello, I was introduced to the two men's partners, and made small talk. It could only be a matter of time, I figured, before the main topic was reached. But it came down to me to raise it.

"No Tel, then?"

"No, he's away, apparently. Due back next week..."

If Paul knew anything about why the master of the house was away when his wife was hosting a drinks afternoon, he wasn't letting on. Conversation drifted back almost immediately to plans for Christmas. It wasn't until much later that I found anything out.

The rest of the afternoon disappeared in a haze of bottom-sniffing, making lightweight talk with some of the Martins' neighbours and friends, watching the others. As I worked my way through a plate of finger snack I looked out of the dining room window, across a perfectly flat and evenly-cut expanse of rich green lawn, towards the wall that I'd used as my entry point a few weeks previously.

Gradually, as the afternoon turned to evening and the lights came and the curtains were drawn, people began to drift away. Paul, Clive and their wives went together – I figured they'd all come together in a single car – and others also gradually finished the last of their drinks and went home.

"Thank God they've nearly all gone. Boring people. Come and sit here and talk to me."

There were only two of us left in the lounge, although others were still in the kitchen. Lianne Martin patted the cushion of the two-seater Chesterfield on which she was perched. I did as I was told.

"So why are you on your own? Wife not come?"

"What wife?"

"The lady with you at the Dorchester. I thought she was your wife."

"No, just a friend. See each other every few weeks or so. But I'm not married, Never have been."

"I'd have thought somebody would have snapped you up–"

"No chance."

We were interrupted by the last two couples, neighbours, the ones who'd been standing in the kitchen, declaring that they were heading home. I watched the shape of her legs as Lianne walked towards the door to see off her guests. As she came back across the room, turning down the lights as she passed the switch. She kicked off her stilettos and sat back down, close enough for me to feel the warmth of her thigh against my own.

“What’s that you’re drinking?”

“Orange juice. I’m driving–”

“Pity. I’ve some really good Polish vodka” – She pronounced it Wodka – “Why don’t you try one?”

“Love to, but like I said, I’m driving–”

“You don’t have to.”

“Eh?”

“You don’t have to. I’ve got loads of room. Stay over. I Don’t feel like being on my own.” Before I had chance to answer she stood, strode across to the shelf unit on the far wall, and poured two shots into tall, thin glasses from a cheap-looking bottle with a simple red and white label. “Light me a cigarette.”

“Sorry, didn’t realise you smoked.”

“Good vodka, eh? I get it sent over from my brother, who still lives in Warzawa.”

“You pronounced it like a native–”

“I was. Once.”

“You don’t have any accent–”

“It went. With my background. I left when I was seventeen. Haven’t been back since, not even for my parents’ funerals.”

Over the course of the next hour we sat alongside each other. I learned that Leonore Wraclew had been helped out of her homeland in the early seventies. She’d made her way across the border into East Germany, where she’d stayed for a few months before making it to the west, crossing in the forest near Wolfsburg. She arrived in London in 1973 and reinvented herself.

“But how–?”

“Don’t ask. Let’s just say I had something that people wanted.”

“I thought that Tel would be here.”

“He’s away. Until the middle of the week. I’m getting hungry. Let’s eat.”

We faced each other across the dining table, hoovering up canapés and finger snacks, and talking. About mutual acquaintances, about the economy, about where I live, about nothing in particular. Eventually I glanced at my watch, and realised that it was almost midnight. She noticed.

“I’ll show you to your room.”

I followed Lianne upstairs, watching the way her long red-painted fingernails trailed along the edge of the light oak of the handrail. She opened the door to a room on the right hand side, and stood in the door frame so that I had to brush alongside her the enter the room.

"There's a bathroom in there if you want a ..." she pointed to a door alongside the white-linened double bed, said "see you later" and left the room, closing the door behind her.

Ten minutes under the shower helped wash away the slight fog that had enveloped me, the result of mixing neat Polish Spirit and my half of a bottle of Rioja reserva. Plus whatever else I already drunk earlier in the day. I pulled on a white towelling robe that was hanging on the back of the door and walked back into the bedroom. Lianne was reclining on the top of the bed wearing nothing but a black bra, matching lacy briefs and black stockings. And a beguiling expression. My jaw hit the middle of my chest.

As I drove through the misty murk of rural Essex the next morning I wondered if I'd just been given a clue to what Lianne had used to get out of Poland. Or maybe it was just an early Christmas present? Whatever, seems that Janice's instinct had been right about Lianne. I was snapped out of wondering by a Renault Espace that ambled out of a driveway into my path, its driver distracted by the brat in the back seat. I swerved out of her way and carried on towards the M25 and home.

My mobile rang an hour and a half later, as I was approaching the Stokenchurch cutting.

"Sutherland. Your man's car has been spotted in the car park of a hotel near the quayside at Poole."

"I was told he'd gone away for a few days, and that he's due back the middle of this week..."

"Thanks for letting me know–"

"I only found out yesterday."

"What's he doing?"

"No idea, just that he's been away for a few days and that he's due back this week."

Sutherland went on to tell me that his local people would be keeping an eye on the car, and would let him know when it moved. He'd keep me informed. I told him who'd been at the Martin's house, but left out details about my sleeping arrangements. None of his business.

Within half an hour of hanging up I pulled up alongside the caravan, dragged my always-ready overnight bag off the back seat so that I could change its contents for next time I needed it, and unlocked the door. Weird shit; I must have forgotten to deadlock it. The door was only on its Yale.

I had the feeling that somebody had been in. Nothing concrete, no apparent signs of disturbance, just an uneasy feeling. I opened a couple of cupboards, the ones over the bench where I keep my current work, and everything looked just as I'd left it on Sunday morning. Lifted the bench up. Moved a half dozen old newspapers off the top and looked at the safe, which again looked untouched. I unlocked it, flicked through the folder of background stuff and the pics for the Tel Martin story, and again nothing seemed to have been touched. The Zip disk was still there, too. I switched on my computer, and loaded the disk; everything was as it ought to be. But I still felt uneasy. Finally, I opened up the Martin file on the hard drive and looked at it.

Again, scrolling through it nothing looked any different. Finally I opened up the Summary Information Statistics subfile. Last saved 16:12:1998 at 03:23. Last night, while I had been sleeping alongside Lianne Martin in the guest bedroom of their house. Shit. I wish I'd picked up one of those wireless alarm systems that I'd seen when I bought the new lock.

I rang Nigel Sutherland. He ought to know, to be told. "Mark McDermott. I had visitors last night."

"Were you there? Why didn't you mention it earlier?"

"I was away last night, as you know. just got back."

"Sorry, must've missed that. Any damage? Anything missing?"

"Nothing. Whoever did it was a pro, could hardly tell that they'd been in. I only know because my computer told me..."

I then had to explain the checks I'd made, and that I hadn't come back home after the drinks party. But I stopped short of telling him with whom I had spent the night.

"And was your stay, erm, planned?"

"No, it just sort of happened."

"And who else knew?"

"Nobody, so far as I was aware."

"Stevenson's by far the most likely. Could he have known that you would be away all night...?"

"Doubt it. Although–"

"Although what?"

"Although he was at the same drinks party as me yesterday afternoon."

After ringing off I wandered across the yard to say hello to Hilda, who'd waved to me through the window. I decided to say nothing about my visitors, unless she did – and the chances were she wouldn't. If whoever had visited my place had been as thorough as I suspected, neither Hilda, Alf, or even Shep the dog would have been aware of their presence.

I spent the better part of the day in a haze of restlessness. I tried sorting out a couple of bits of work, and abandoned it. Opened the post, and finding nothing riveting in there shoved it into a drawer. I tried playing my guitar for a while, taking a stab at some old Peter Green licks from his Fleetwood Mac period, but gave up on it. I was sounding more like an injured duck than an *Albatross.*

Then I went for a walk across the fields. A thin and watery sun breaking through the gloom of the December day was enough to persuade me. So I pulled on my fleece-lined Ford Rally Team coat and strolled towards the woods and back again. The silver grey of the grass crunched underfoot along the path. And all the time my head was filled with shadowy images of a dark-clothed bloke ferreting through my caravan, of memories of last night with Lianne, of getting pulverised by Tel's heavies if he ever found out, of Mike lying with a caved-in skull. I Wished I'd taken my Walkman. Some music would've been a distraction.

My mobile rang as I was crossing the lane back to home. Lianne's number came up as the caller identity.

"Hi, it's me. You got back allright, then?"

"Yes, thanks, was home before lunch–"

"Do you fancy meeting me for a bite in town later this week? I'm going up West to do some last-minute shopping and–"

"Yeah, that'd be great. I'd enjoy that. But won't Tel be back by then? Won't that cause–"

"No it won't. Do you know Shepherd Market? There's a nice little bistro there. On the left as it opens out, as you go from Park Lane. See you there at about one?"

And she was gone. As I picked up the Stratocaster again it occurred to me. A week ago the idea of screwing Lianne Martin was about the last thing I'd have considered. She's maybe five years older than me, but that's not the issue; she's married to a bloke that I'm investigating. Not to mention the police, the Customs & Excise, and God knows who else. I put a Santana CD in the deck and jammed along to it, finding a kind of oblivion by getting lost in the LA-Latino rhythms.

12

Open and closed books

Sutherland rang me again on Wednesday morning.

"He's just picked up his car. He was dropped there by a female in a light blue Mercedes–"

"A sporty one?"

"Yes. How did you know?"

"Just an inspired guess."

"Anyway, the car had just driven off the overnight ferry from Guernsey–"

"Was that where they'd been all week?"

"Apparently so. Unless they'd flown out of the Island; her car was logged into Guernsey last Wednesday, and stayed there, so far as we know. Our colleagues at the Bureau are checking flight manifests, but we reckon–"

"That he'd been seeing his bankers? Or just a week of passion with his bit on the side?"

"One or the other. Whatever. Anyway, thought I'd let you know."

So Tel probably had bought a matched pair of Mercedes coupés. I pondered for a moment why he should need to screw around when he's got a passionate and sensual woman like Lianne at home, then thought again. If everything was right, she wouldn't have screwed me, wouldn't be contemplating screwing me again. Other peoples' marriages are a closed book. I think it was Claire Rayner who said that... Or Maybe it wasn't. Whoever it was, she was right.

And now that Tel was back in town other things might crank up a gear. I opened the cellophane wrapper around another Zip disk and backed up the entire contents of my hard drive. This went in a brown envelope with all the photographs. I sealed it, then put it into a padded envelope with a covering note. I drove down to the Post Office and sent the package by recorded delivery to Paul Laker at his office. If anybody could be trusted to keep it safe he could.

I took an early train down to town, and then hammered my credit card on Oxford Street buying presents for my parents, and for Hilda and Alf. As I turned the corner from Queen Street I spotted a long, slender-ankled, high-heeled leg stepping out of a black cab.

"What a lovely day!" She turned her head to the side for me to kiss her cheek.

The waitress took her coat and the close-fitting fur hat that she removed from her head as soon as we sat. Around her shoulders was a blue silk scarf that probably cost twice as much as the suede jacket I was wearing. Its colour picked up on the fine check of her dress.

"You look wonderful."

She glanced across at me with the half smile of a woman used to receiving compliments. Then she turned her attention to the menu written on a blackboard to the side of the small plain wood bar.

"What have you…" Lianne paused as the waiter arrived to take our drinks order, and handed us a pair of folders containing the menu. Then she continued "what have you planned of the afternoon?"

"Nothing, why?"

"Good."

I looked to her for a reply, but she just smiled.

The waiter returned, and stood patiently for three or four minutes, long enough for us both to scan the choices and select starters and main courses.

"Merry Christmas." She eventually tilted her glass of wine towards me. Then glanced towards the handful of carrier bags to the side of my chair. "So, what have you been buying?"

"Oh, just a couple of bits and pieces for my parents and for some friends–"

"Your girlfriend? What have you bought for her?"

"You know I don't have one. Not a regular one, anyway. Not regular enough to justify buying a Christmas present for– "

"So tell me about her–"

"Who says there's just the one?"

I was retrieved from the situation by our starter course arriving. By the time that the waiter had finished flourishing his enormous pepper mill I felt safe to change the subject.

"So what have you been buying? You don't seem to have many bags…"

"Nothing yet. Been into Harvey Nicks for some clothes, but they're all being altered. They'll deliver them. Got Terry's present weeks ago, and there's nobody else–"

"Not even me?"

She smiled enigmatically. "Later."

The lights in the distance caught the raindrops that streamed along the side windows of the train as it headed back towards Oxford. From lunch I'd been whisked straight off to a hotel, a smart, chi-chi designer place across the far side of Park Lane, just across the road from the Georgian mansion that houses the motor industry's 'trade union' headquarters. She'd already booked the room, and paid for it with a gold card while I stood and waited. She was handed a key, and declined the offer of help from a porter to take us up to the room.

"No, we'll find our own way, thanks."

Two minutes later we were two floors up, in our room. After helping her remove her coat she'd unclipped and removed her scarf, and asked me to unzip her dress. I felt my groin stir, recalling the sensations from that first time, enjoying the delicious anticipation as the dress parted to reveal her naked back.

"So this is my Christmas present, then?" I'd stroked a fingertip along the ridge of her spine as she lay, face down and relaxing after a passionate burst of sexual frenzy, alongside me on the uncovered bed.

She turned her head and smiled at me. "Light me a cigarette. And there's a hip flask in my bag. Be a darlink and pass it to me."

I looked down at her slim, long body as I walked back across from the table. "There aren't any glasses, only tumblers in the bathroom."

"The French drink brandy out of tumblers."

She reached into her bag and pulled out a silver flask, flipped the lock hinge expertly, and poured slugs of liquid into the two glasses I'd put down on the bedside table. Then she hit me with the line that was echoing in my mind as I watched the raindrops trace a line along the windows of the carriage. And that would still haunt me months later.

"I'm thinking about dumping him."

She wouldn't be drawn any further. We drank our brandy, smoked our cigarettes, and screwed again, this time less urgently. An hour later we were out of the hotel. She got into a cab and I walked off towards the underground at Hyde Park Corner. She said she's ring me later.

"Thank you. Can we open them now? Want a cuppa?"

Hilda sat across the kitchen table, with the unmatched pair of gift-wrapped parcels in front of her.

"No thanks, just had a coffee. No, leave them 'til Christmas day. Then you can give me your undying gratitude when I get back from Mum and Dad's."

"Yours is over there. And I can tell you now, you'd better get saving. There'll be three of us this time next year."

'What?"

"I'm expecting. Not 'til next June, but..."

I walked around the table and kissed her on the cheek. "Congratulations! I was beginning to think Alf didn't have it in him!"

"Cheeky sod! You'd better not let him hear you say that! Don't forget he always has a couple of shells in the shotgun–"

"No really, I'm delighted for you, both of you. Oh, did I tell you that I've put an alarm system in the caravan? After that visit a while back I've been meaning to get one, so I picked one up yesterday. It's wire free, and flashes a blue light inside when the siren goes off. Hopefully I won't need it, but just in case you hear it, you'll know what it... what all the noise is. Here's the code, just key this number in to switch it off and put it in again to put it back on. It gives you thirty seconds to get out..."

I told her where the keypad was fixed, scribbled the digits on a piece of paper and pushed it across the table to Hilda, then said goodbye and walked back across the yard to finish packing. The answering machine was flashing when I got back into the caravan, and there was a 'missed call' message in the screen of my mobile, too.

"Hi, it's Mark Mc..."

"Thanks for getting back to me so quickly. I thought I might have missed you. Are you away for Christmas?"

"Yeah, will be, just down to my parents' place. Back the day after Boxing Day."

"Our Dutch friends have arrested the man with the limp, van Drel. Watched him for a while and then picked him up at dawn. He's not saying anything, though, apparently..."

"What about the British end? You any nearer arrests there?"

"Keeping a watching brief. We did, however, liberate the last two containers from a house in West Ten, where they ended up. Replaced them with an identical pair full of baking soda. Rather surprised that the shit hasn't hit the fan yet. Somebody will be very upset that they've been–"

"Maybe van Drel's safer inside. Otherwise they might be out to get him."

Sutherland laughed. "Yes, perhaps. Anyway, thought I'd bring you up to speed. Are you on your mobile in case anything develops?"

"Yeah, I'm only on the south coast. They have mobile phone services down there, you know... But I'll give you my folks number in case the signals are down. They sometimes get blocked by the military..."

We left it that unless something major happened I would speak to him again after the holidays. I packed a bag, and put it and the presents for my parents into the car. I also packed the couple of bottles of decent Bordeaux that had arrived by post a few days earlier, a 'thank you' from Ray Otley. I was about to lock up the caravan when a white courier's van pulled up alongside my idling Rover.

"Package for you, mate."

I signed the sheet, and took the jiffy bag off him.

"All the best, mate."

"Yeah, cheers, and you."

I got into the car and opened the package. Inside was a slim, gift-wrapped parcel with a gift tag that read 'Merry Christmas. Here's to Next Time! L.' Peeling off the wrapping paper exposed a black leather-look box embossed with the Rado logo. Opening it revealed a very chic wristwatch with simple black face and fine barred silver strap. Worth at least a grand, maybe more. I snapped the lid shut and slipped the box into my inside pocket. Then selected first gear, turned the wheel and headed for Sandbanks and a quiet couple of days.

13
Family fortunes

"You look well."

"Thanks, Dad, you're looking pretty good yourself. Mum not around?" I realised that his age was starting to show. For the first time in my life I was taller than he was. Not by much, maybe a half inch, but taller. He was starting to shrink from his original five eleven, starting the regression that comes from being on the wrong side of sixty.

"She'll be back anytime. Had to pop out to pick up the vegetables, apparently. Drink?"

I kicked off my shoes and stretched out in the familiar surroundings of the lounge, looking out through open curtains towards the sea, which was almost impossible to discern in the fading light. I relaxed easily in this house where I'd spent most of my teenage years.

Dad and I talked about trade, about how the grain industry was suffering, like all food businesses, at the hands of supermarkets perpetually looking at ways of improving their margins. As we talked – or more accurately as I listened to Dad's concept of moving more into animal feed from human food – I appreciated how lucky I'd been. Lucky in getting out of the constant offers to get involved, in doing my own thing. For a couple of years this had been a problem, partly because my earnings as a cub reporter were appallingly low, and partly because I had to work a lot of anti-social hours.

So far as my parents were concerned I could walk straight into a better salary and an easier working week, and they had difficulty getting their heads around the fact that I would put up with everything because I wanted to be a journalist. It wasn't until I started writing books, until I could put something into their hands that they could touch and see that I had created from nothing, that things started to change. The turning point came when I'd gone home one weekend for a family party to celebrate one of Aunt Celia's occasional visits from California. I overheard my father showing Celia, his only sister, my first book, and telling how proud he was that it was not only in existence, but was dedicated with love and thanks to Mum and Dad. From that point onwards there were no references to me joining McDermott Grain Millers.

We sat opposite each other in the lounge. "What about retirement, Dad?"

"What about it? Your mother complains now at the weekends, says I'm always cluttering the place up. Even suggested I take up golf..."

Mum arrived home just as I drained the last drops of my first beer from its glass.

"Hello darling, you're here early. Are you hungry? I could sort you a sandwich..."

Five minutes later I sat at the kitchen table demolishing a ham and mustard baguette. A fresh beer appeared in my glass.

"Hilda told me that they're expecting a baby next summer–"

"Wonderful! Hope she doesn't have any complications. She's getting on a bit for her first–"

"She's only thirty eight, Mum, the same age as me–"

"Yes dear, I know how old you are. I don't suppose there's any sign of you settling down, though... Anyway, thirty eight is quite old to be having her first child."

I was saved from a lecture about assuming responsibility – or more accurately providing my mother with a grandchild – by my mobile ringing. Mum shot me an exasperated look as I left the half-eaten sandwich and moved through to the dining room to take the call.

"Hi. Did you get your present? Do you like it?"

"It's absolutely wonderful – but you shouldn't have. I feel really guilty that I didn't get you anything–"

"Oh, I thought it was the right thank you for what you gave me at the Halkin–"

"Lianne!"

She laughed. She was obviously alone. And I could feel myself going red, like I hadn't done in years. "Are you on your own through the holiday?"

"No such luck. He's gone to pick up another bottle of brandy. Got a bloody houseful until Sunday. Are you wearing it?"

"Not yet. I need to adjust the strap–"

"No excuse for being late, now, have you?"

"Me, late? Never."

"You better not be either– Tel's pulling up. Better go. Ring you beginning of next week. Keep your diary open. Bye."

I wandered back into the kitchen, where Mum was busy putting away the last of her shopping.

"Your girlfriend?"

"Mum..."

"You might be the one with the sophisticated life, but you can't fool your mother–"

"Just a friend, Mum. Honest. If there's any prospect of you becoming a grandmother..." I ducked to avoid a flying sprout. "Your aim's improving!"

I sat in my bedroom. The walls were still covered with framed prints of racing greats from the late seventies; Tambay, a signed Fittipaldi, Brambilla, Arnoux. Model cars on the bookshelves, a stack of old magazines. Pretty much as it had always been. I didn't bother unpacking my bag, just hung it like a cloth wardrobe on the hook behind the door. Do all mothers leave their only sons' rooms as a shrine to a distant childhood?

I flipped open the box and took out the watch, slipped off my old Seiko and fastened the expensive piece of designer hardware in its place. It was a bit loose – Dad'd have a tool somewhere that I could use to alter it. As I took it off I flipped it over and saw that the back was inscribed:

Mark
Happy Christmas
L
1998

I reached for my mobile, and got as far as scrolling to the last received number. But decided that ringing at eight thirty on Christmas Eve wasn't the smartest idea. I'd be speaking to her again in a few days anyway. Wonder if my new watch was bought using Marsport's charge card?

My mobile rang as I was driving up the hill out of Salisbury.

"Hi, it's me. Have a nice Christmas?"

"Lovely, thanks. Quiet, but enjoyable."

"Can you get into town on Thursday? Be nice to see you."

"Yeah, that'd be great. Where?

"Same place, Shepherd Market, about one?"

We left it that I'd see her at the bistro. I smiled in anticipation, and carried on heading towards Swindon. Not much after lunchtime I pulled into the yard alongside my caravan. Alf was walking across the lane, a shotgun in the crook of his arm and a half dozen woodpigeons hanging upside down in his other hand. He'd already waved them at me as I turned into the gateway.

"Hi Mark, how're your folks?"

"Great, thanks. How was your Christmas?"

"Good, thanks, come over for a coffee. We'll fill you in."

I put my bag, and a carrier holding the sweater and blouson that I'd been given by my parents, in the caravan. Paused to flick the gas fire on. Then went back to the car and took a couple of wrapped presents off the back seat, and walked across to the farmhouse. I let myself into the kitchen door. I put the presents down on the dresser, explaining that they were from Mum and Dad. Hilda already had my coffee ready on the large oak table.

"I told them your news. They were delighted. Or at least Mum was, you know what Dad's like, never says much."

I know. She's already been on this morning to congratulate us... That's nice, did they buy you that?" She was pointing towards the new watch wrapped around my left wrist.

"No, this was from a friend."

"Some friend! Not exactly a fiver off the market stuff, is it? She someone special?"

"Who says it's she?"

"If it's not a woman, then we've got problems. They don't like pooftahs around these parts, do they Alf?"

Alf laughed as he walked across the room and sat down. "Your alarm thing went off last night. No one about, though. Went over, but the place was all locked up proper."

"Took his bloody gun with him, and all. Keep telling him, one of these days he'll get into trouble... You tell him Mark–"

"She's probably right, Alf. But I reckon I'd do the same..."

Hilda disappeared up the stairs. As soon as he heard the floorboards in the room above us creak, Alf stood and went over to the corner, picking up a long brown bag and coming back. He slid the bag across the table.

"Here, you can have this. A mate of mine gave it to me a couple of weeks back. Better get a licence, though. And you'll have to have a proper cupboard in to hold it."

I unzipped the side of the bag and pulled out a double-barrelled twelve bore. There was a small red box of cartridges in the bottom of the bag. As I studied it I asked Alf "Couldn't I keep it here?"

"The whole point is that you have it. Handy. You're making some strange friends and..."

I nodded. Hilda came back down as Alf was explaining the protocol for getting a shotgun licence, adding that I'd have no problems. "Make sure they know its a farm when you give them your address. Tell them you just use it for a bit of recreational shooting, helping me keep vermin down..."

The look on Hilda's face was that she didn't approve.

I had been sat in the bistro for about ten minutes, nursing a coffee and glancing at the newspaper I'd taken from the rack by the bar, when Lianne arrived. I stood, kissed her on both cheeks, then settled her into her chair before sitting back down.

"You look lovely."

"Thank you. You're looking very smart yourself."

Anticipating the way she would look like a million dollars, I'd taken the precaution of wearing a suit. The suit. And a new black roll-neck sweater. "Thought I'd better make an effort–"

"I'm honoured. You're wearing it, then..." Her eyes had fixed momentarily on my left wrist.

"Of course. And I was ten minutes early–"

"No you weren't. It was me being ten minutes late."

We laughed, and settled back to order lunch.

A couple of hours later we were in a room at the same hotel. Again, she paid. Again I helped her undress, and again the initial urgency was intense. This was followed by a calmer, more relaxed, screw. We stretched out on the bed in between, drinking brandy and smoking. Her phone rang, but she flipped it open, pressed the red button and put it down again.

"Terry. He can wait." Then she started to stroke me with the red nail of her index finger, tracing a line down from the middle of my chest. Tel was forgotten. I asked her later where he thought she would be.

"At the sales."

"But you haven't bought anything."

"Self-obsessed bastard wouldn't notice. And anyway, he'll be out when I get back."

14
Foreign affairs

"You fancy coming to Estoril with us next week?" Ray's call came as I was driving back from the police station in Oxford the next morning, from taking in my shotgun licence application.

"Yeah, that'd be good. What are the arrangements?"

"Get over here early. Seven, Tuesday morning. Got a private plane chartered, going from Kidlington at half eight. We'll be back Wednesday at about eight. Sort you a room at our hotel."

The weekend disappeared into a whirlwind of writing, putting down the feature ideas that had occurred to me when I had been walking along the harbourside at Poole on Boxing Day. I'd scribbled them down as I sat in the bar of a pub just off the quay. I fired off a couple of messages to editors, and settled back reading through what I'd already committed to text on the Tel Martin book. Nigel Sutherland rang on Sunday morning.

"Thought you might be amused to learn that a couple of heavies turned up at the address in Maastricht, looking for van Drel. Even though he's not there his place is still under surveillance. They wired over a picture to us, and it was almost certainly the two that we're already looking for. We'd already tipped the Dutch off that they were on their way. According to our contacts these two were apparently not terribly happy. I suspect that they'd opened up the containers and reckoned that it was the Dutchman that had conned them. Apparently they caught up with van Drel's people and gave them a hard time."

"I presume that he's still–"

"Very much so. They've moved him, put him in a high security facility they have up in the North. For his own safety, according to our colleagues there–"

"Sounds like he needs it... Don't you ever take any time off, by the way?"

"What?"

"It's Sunday. Most people are tucked up at home–"

"Most of my colleagues are. I'm divorced, though, so I'd sooner work than stare at the walls of my flat."

"Has there been any news about Mike Lewis?"

"Not heard anything. Inspector Granville was all on for pulling in Martin, but my superiors persuaded him that it wouldn't be in the national interest, and that he ought to leave it to our friends in the SCS. So I presume he's still sulking–"

"SCS?"

"Serious Crime Squad. Sorry, bad habit of mine, presuming that everybody is familiar with the shorthand."

He rang off, but ten minutes later was back on.

"I've just spoken to a Sergeant Greene at Oxford, works alongside Granville. Seems they've had a result.

He explained that they'd arrested a man, steaming drunk, between Christmas and New Year. They'd thrown him in a cell to sober up, and started the routine questioning once he was in a fit state. And he had blurted out that he'd got involved with a scrap in the small hours last July that had ended up with your friend lying on a slab in the mortuary.

"So there was no connection between him and Tel Martin?"

"None whatsoever."

Ray sat alongside me on the little Embraer jet as we passed over the coast of Brittany and out towards the Bay of Biscay.

"Did you know they'd made an arrest for Mike Lewis's murder?

"Somebody said something this morning. Seems it was in the Citizen last weekend. Meant to ask you if you'd heard–"

"Never bother reading the local paper. Apparently it was all over some girl that Mike had been screwing. Seems her boyfriend got the hump and went round to sort him out. Lost it completely and went right over the top. According to the plod he'll be up for manslaughter. Should come to trial by about the middle of the year."

We were interrupted by the stewardess bringing breakfast. As we sat and ate our croissants at thirty thousand feet, I couldn't help but feel deflated. And a little exposed. If it hadn't been for Mike I'd never have picked up on the Tel Martin drug connection, and I'd never have been screwing Lianne. I'd convinced myself that Mike being killed was connected to Tel, but had been about as wrong as I could have been. And decided that I was too far in to stop now.

"Women. Always bloody trouble, eh mate?"

I glanced at my wrist, at the expensive gift from Lianne, and back at Ray. "Yeah, dead right..."

We stepped off the aircraft into a bright, warm day. I searched out my sunglasses from the side pocket of the camera bag slung over my shoulder.

"Bit better than back home, eh Mark?"

"Certainly is. Took me nearly ten minutes to get the ice off the car this morning. Seems like another world."

I walked alongside Pat Kearns, fishing my passport from the inside pocket of my jacket as we crossed the tarmac.

"Been upsetting anybody lately?"

"Eh?"

"Don't tell me you've forgotten already. Silverstone, blood, blokes in Land Rover–"

"Oh, right. No, been good."

"Ever work out why?"

"I was getting a bit close to somebody. You'll find out as soon as it's safe to tell–"

"Sounds like I'm better off not knowing."

"Yeah, maybe."

We were interrupted by having to pass through the immigration desk. By the time I emerged from the passageway Pat was already disappearing, in search of the minibus that was due to collect us from outside the airport and take us along the circuit.

An hour later I was sitting on the grey concrete wall separating the pitlane from the track. Sipping fresh coffee and watching one car at a time put in a couple of laps against a backdrop of empty grandstand seats and then pull back in for more tweaking. Enjoying the howl of thoroughbred engines. Appreciating the warmth of the sun on my back. I looked across towards the Marsport pit. Their race car pulled out of its garage, got a last minute check from its engineer, and headed off down the pitlane towards the track.

Paul Stevenson walked across and leaned over the wall, ready to watch his car pass a couple of moments later. I heard the rise and fall of its engine note as the driver worked the car through the curves behind me, and a few seconds on it burst into view. It slid out to the rumble strips around the exit of Parabolica, then hooked up and blasted onto the long straight. It was plain grey, bright and shiny new, but wearing no decals whatsoever. I strolled the thirty yards along the walkway and joined Stevenson.

"Hi Paul, how's it going?"

"Good. Very good." His expression told me to fuck off and stop bothering him, but I ignored it and continued.

"Engine sounds strong. New one?"

"Just testing it out. Cosworth development unit. Should be strong enough, but you know what this game's like. Fine until you put them into a race then something magic happens. Still, happy with it so far–"

He was interrupted by a squawk from his personal radio, turned his back to me and talked into the microphone, then turned back, still talking. He nodded to me and went back across to the garage, followed into it by the race car. I followed.

I stood at the entrance of the garage, alongside the nose of the now-silent car, and watched as Paul Williams extracted himself from the confines of the cockpit.

He unplugged his radio lead and pulled off his crash helmet. "Happy New Year, mate. You're looking fit. What the secret? I've put a bit of weight on over the break." He patted his stomach and smirked at me, then turned away and went into a huddle with Paul and Tel.

I hadn't seen Tel arrive. I strolled back down the lane to the GTD garage and helped myself to another coffee from the insulated jug on a bench at the back.

"When's the book due out?" Tel and I sat in the lounge of the Estoril Palace hotel, the only stragglers left. Everybody else seemed to have gone to bed early.

"Spring list, but that probably means May or June, publishing has a calendar all of its own. Occupies a nice little parallel universe. Last year I got a call from a publisher who wanted to see me urgently to talk about a book idea. Then made me wait three weeks to get together with him. We were threequarters of the way through lunch before we even got round to discussing the project. It's that sort of business."

"Have you actually finished it yet?"

Shit. How do I tell him that I'm waiting for him to get arrested and up in court before I can wrap up the last chapter? "Nearly. Just a few bits and pieces to put into the first draft, then it goes into my publishers for editing and typesetting. Should get it into them by the end of the month."

Tel seemed happy with this. He drained his glass and looked at mine. "Refill?"

"Cheers. One for the gutter..."

He called over the waiter clearing empties from the table by the door, and ordered two brandies – no ice. We made small talk, about what we'd done over the break, about the car, about the new season.

"You've got no sponsorship showing. Any plans yet?"

"Never livery up before the start of the season, you should know that." He lied. His cars had always appeared at test sessions in full sponsorship colours, even when they were straight-out-of-the-box new. Even when the sponsorship deal was still in pencil. It was one of his tricks, shaming new sponsors into signing up by showing them how the car will look on the tracks, and suggesting that they couldn't pull out now because it would reflect badly on them. He probably never went as far as saying to shaky sponsors that he'd make sure that the blame was attached to them. He probably didn't need to be so explicit. It's his understanding of that psychology that has made him such a formidable force in the racing industry.

"That new engine sounded good. So you're sticking with Cosworth, then?"

"Yes, of course. Worked with them for so long, always reliable, good people to deal with..."

I went to bed. Drifted off thinking about Lianne, and also thinking that I ought to give Janice a ring. No sense having all my eggs in one basket...

We exchanged pleasantries again the next day, Tel and I. As we stood in the pitlane, watching the recovery truck pull in with his race car on the back I looked for some kind of indicator, but his face was expressionless.

"What's happened?"

"Nothing major. He's wrecked the gearbox, from the sound of it. Wish we had telemetry like they have in F1. That way our guys would have been able to stop him, or at least warn him before he broke it–"

"This down to the new engine?"

"Not really. Doubt it, anyway. Pure transmission problem."

"Early bath?"

"Only an hour to go in the session, and we were wrapping up tonight anyway. No great problem."

"So you flying out tonight?"

"Yeah, plane's ready whenever I am. How about you? Who've you come down with, anyway?"

"GTD. Don't forget I've known Ray Otley for a long time..."

Tel wandered off into the back of the pit. His relaxed demeanour was for my benefit; the chances were high that Paul Williams would be getting his balls chewed off for breaking a fifty grand gearbox, for not stopping when he first picked up the warning signs, the noises that should have told him something was wrong.

I ambled back down the quiet pitlane to the GTD garage. They were getting their car ready for a last couple of laps as soon as the marshals reopened the track. As I nodded to Ray, who stood at the back of the car, the engine burst into life with a deafening crack, then settled down to a rumble that was just noisy. Ray walked out as the car pulled out onto the tarmac.

"You ready for off at five?"

"Yeah, no worries."

"Been worthwhile?"

"Definitely. Get a nice piece off this. I like it when I'm the only hack on the scene."

"Sounds like you owe me another drink..."

15

A bleak midwinter

I was back into the freezing January of the English home counties by ten that night. As I de-iced the car I wished I could figure a way of being able to live in a Mediterranean country – or failing that Portugal – for the winter. I told Janice about this when I saw her the following Sunday.

"So that's where you bleedin' disappeared to then, was it?"

"Only for a couple of day midweek. Out of season testing."

"My heart goes out to you."

"So what'd you do over Christmas? And didn't I even qualify for a card?"

"Was going to send you one, but... Anyway, where was mine, you bastard?"

"Must have got lost in the post ..."

She laughed, a tinkling sound that became a snort. We ate lunch in a pub around the corner from her house, and made small talk.

"What've you got planned for later?"

"Nothing. You any ideas? Movie or something?"

"That's dangerously close to normal. We'll see what's on when we go back to my place..."

We ended up at the theatre, watching an excellent cast's interpretation of Priestley's *An Inspector Calls* in the West End, followed by a late night pasta supper in a little Italian place just off Charing Cross Road. Then back to Janice's for a riotously horny night.

I drove home on Monday morning feeling good. The sunlight was bright and harsh, illuminating the silver frosted green of the fields either side of the M40. I glanced across at the snake of cars heading into London on the other carriageway and decided I'd earned myself an easy day.

I went via Oxford to pick up the rolls of film I'd taken in Estoril, then back home and over the lightbox. I flicked though the sheets of images and cut out the best ones, binning any that were out of focus. Half of what I kept went into an envelope and off to Auto Racing, and the others I got ready for mailing to Motorsport News. I'd already filed the copy, and between the two features they'd pay all the bills for the month with a bit of cash to spare. Neat. I zipped down to Wheatley, sent off the packages, then went across the road to the mini-mart to get some bread and milk.

There was a police car waiting as I pulled back into the yard. An ordinary little Astra containing a sergeant who grunted as he extracted his bulk from the confined space between the wheel and his seat. The suspension of the car seemed to sigh as it was unburdened.

"Mr McDermott? Alf told me you were due back anytime. Not a problem, it's about your licence application."

"Licence?" My thoughts went to my driving licence, tucked away somewhere in my wallet.

"Shotgun licence. Need to see where you're going to keep the gun..."

"Ah, of course. Sorry."

I unlocked the door, and keyed the code into the alarm pad to stop it bleeping. I offered the policeman a drink as I persuaded the gas fire into life. He declined.

"No thanks, got to get back. It's almost dinner time."

He poked about, inspected the padlock on the secure cupboard that Alf had helped me put under the bench seat alongside the safe. Scribbled a couple of notes on the clipboard dwarfed by his enormous hands.

"Do you keep cash in there?" He pointed at the safe.

"No, just work. Backup discs, that sort of thing..."

The sergeant nodded approvingly, asked about where I would be keeping the key to the padlock that I would be using to lock the gun box. How often the gun would be likely to be used, and seeking an assurance that I would keep the cartridges separate. "If there's room in your safe, that'd be the best place for 'em..." and concluded that he had no problem signing off my application. My certificate should arrive in the next few days, then I could get a gun. I didn't have the heart to tell him I already owned a Browning side-by-side...

Then he revised his decision about a drink, and spent the next half hour telling me how he thought all these racing drivers and footballers and movie stars were overpaid and they ought to try his job. Then realised that he was into his lunch break zone and scuttled off as quickly as his considerable bulk and overall lack of fitness would allow.

The licence arrived by the end of the week, so Alf and I celebrated by going shooting woodpigeon. He showed me how to use a shotgun, aiming with both eyes rather than just one, like you would with a rifle. And how to tuck the stock back to reduce the bruising. It was a bit late for that; three days later my right shoulder was still blue and tender to the touch – but I could hit the things I aimed at. And I was getting quite good at fast aiming.

"Help yourself anytime you fancy some practice." Alf told me, as we walked back across the fields towards home "Just make sure I'm not out there already before you start shooting."

"Your man seems to have gone missing again."

"Not just gone to Guernsey again with his girlfriend?"

"No sign of her. Ever since that particular connection was made our chaps have been keeping a watch for her car at the port–"

"I'll see if I can find anything out. I take it they've looked in the same hotel car park in Poole for Tel's car?"

"Of course. We'd appreciate anything you can dig up, though. You seem able to find out more than we can at times–"

"Just the social circles I mix in, that's all…"

Nigel Sutherland rang off as quickly as he'd started the conversation. With the start of the season still a couple of months off there'd be no need for Tel to be around all the time. I hadn't heard from Lianne in a few days. And it was always possible that they'd gone off to their place in the Canaries. What surprised me about this was that I felt just a little jealous, jealous that Lianne and Tel were enjoying themselves somewhere sunny. Or more accurately that Tel was with Lianne somewhere sunny. I put the thought from my head by strolling across the yard to collect my post, hopefully blagging a cup of tea into the bargain.

"Hate to say this Hilda, but have you considered that you might need to go on a diet?"

She flicked me with the towel she'd been using to dry the breakfast-time pots. "Cheeky sod!" The lump of her forthcoming child was beginning to show.

My mobile rang, deep inside a pocket. I fished it out, and seeing Lianne's number answered. I started to exit the kitchen, waving fingers to Hilda as I went through the door.

"Hi, how are you?"

"Great, thanks, Thought you were away?"

"Whatever gave you that idea? Just been a bit busy. Tried ringing you the other day, but your phone was off and you hadn't put your call-back on…"

"Don't know. Probably a flat battery or something–"

"Not a problem I usually associate with you. Anyway, are you up to anything tomorrow?"

"No, why?"

"Fancy meeting me in town?"

We arranged to meet in a pub on the corner of Arlington Street. "I don't think I'll fancy lunch" she'd told me.

"Aren't you warm in that?" I looked across the table to where Lianne was sitting, sipping her vodka and tonic. She looked down at the mink that was wrapping around her, then back at me, fixing me with sparkling eyes. Today they were more blue than grey.

"I'm fine, thanks. Let's finish these and find a cab."

We walked out of the pub and down to St James's Street, and spotted a cab with its orange light blazing as we turned the corner. Fifteen minutes later we were in our hotel room. She tossed her bags onto the dresser top, pulled off her hat and ran a finger through her hair.

"Now you can help me off with my coat."

I walked behind her and took the shoulders of her fur as she unbuttoned it. No wonder she didn't want to take it off in the pub; all she was wearing underneath it was a fitted red basque, stockings and G-string. She turned around, snaked her arms around my neck, and kissed me hard on the mouth.

"Get your clothes off."

A few minutes later, sated, she stretched out on the bed.

"Do you have to get back tonight?"

"No, why?"

"I always pay for the night in this place. Thought we might get our moneysworth..."

"Won't Tel want to know where you are?"

"No."

The thought jumped back into my mind 'I'm thinking about dumping him.'

"So what do you do for relaxation? Apart from shagging me?"

"I play guitar, go for walks, read–"

"Play guitar? Any good?"

"Brilliantly. Sort of. If it wasn't for a complete lack of talent I could match Jeff Beck or Jimmy Page anytime, note for note–"

"Who are they? Never heard of them."

"That's what happens when you grow up in Rural Poland under communism. You live a deprived existence. Particularly as you're deprived of the best rock guitarists in the world..."

She thumped my shoulder.

We'd spent the evening in a piano bar across the road from the pub we'd been in earlier. A slinky red dress had emerged from her bag, which she'd slipped on after we'd showered together. I looked across at her after the plates were cleared from our table, and the last of the bottle of Merlot poured into our glasses.

"This isn't fair."

"What isn't, darlink?" This was the only word she used that betrayed her middle European origins.

"Knowing that under your dress you're wearing tiny lingerie. And that makes me horny as hell..."

"Well let's pay and go back to the Hotel."

As I watched her walk across towards the cloakroom door, I placed my card on top of the bill. Prayed that it wouldn't reject. Made a mental note to check the balance soon, to try and pay a chunk of it. The waiter returned with the slip, I signed it, helped Lianne pull her fur back on, and we left. Within minutes we were writhing on the bed, still half clothed.

We fell asleep. I slept soundly until almost eight. Then my phone started bleeping. "Sorry, forgot to cancel it. Use it as an alarm... When the chickens don't get to wake me first."

"I'm starved. Let's have something to eat."

From across the breakfast table I plucked up courage to ask the awkward question.

"So where's Tel?"

"Away. For a while. Possibly with that tart."

I was stunned. I wanted to ask how she tolerated the situation, and more importantly, why. But I couldn't bring myself to. Anyway, what she and I got up to wasn't exactly acceptable in some circles. Tel'd probably cave my skull in if he ever found out. We ate on in silence. Eventually she spoke.

"Would you show me where you live?"

"Er, yes, when?"

"Today."

"But I came down on the train..."

"I've got my car in the car park."

"But don't you have to–"

"No. My time's my own. I'm curious to see this caravan of yours."

Within an hour we were tooling down the motorway in her blue Mercedes. I looked across at her, watching the sharp reactions and the positive way in which she drove as we passed streams of cars along the motorway. Only the Phil Collins CD playing in the background detracted from my enjoyment of the moment. I need to educate her, sharpen up her musical tastes.

I directed here off the motorway and along the lanes, and pointed out where to park her car, picking a spot on the hard standing. The last thing she'd thank me for was mud on her stilettos. As she waited for me to unlock the door I was aware of a muted laugh. She'd spotted the house nameplate that I'd ordered on a whim a year or so before. It read *'Sea View'*. I stepped back for her to pass through the door ahead of me.

"It's much nicer than I'd imagined... Play me some of that Jimmy Beck, or whatever his name was–"

"Eh?"

"That guitarist you were telling me about. I'd like to hear some. Jimmy something, wasn't it?"

I put Jeff Beck's *Flash* in the deck, and cranked up the volume. "It's the only way to listen to it..." I shouted above the sound of sharp guitar. She sat on the edge of the cushion behind the table, looking slightly uncomfortable. I turned the volume control back a couple of notches.

"Sorry, don't have much in the way of creature comforts..."

"Looks pretty good. Or at least it will once the place has warmed up."

"Doesn't take long..."

She stood and walked across to look out of the window towards the wood. Picked up a couple of my model racing cars from the shelf and put them down again. Then she ambled off, put her head briefly around the door of the shower room, and carried on into the bedroom. "So how many have you had in here?" She looked at the skewed blue quilt cover then at me. With a smile on her precisely painted scarlet lips that slowly opened to reveal her teeth.

"That'd be telling, wouldn't it?"

She moved across to the bedroom window and closed the blind. Then turned into me and kissed me hard as we twisted and fell onto the bed.

"Bit posh for you, isn't she?" Hilda shot me a glance as she cajoled the ancient Land Rover's gear lever into fourth. "Anyway, why didn't she take you to pick your car up?"

"Completely forgot to ask her. Didn't realise I'd left the car at the station until I was waving her off–"

"Typical. You blokes all have your brains in your Y-Fronts."

Fifteen minutes later we pulled into the car park at Oxford.

"So where is it, then?"

I directed Hilda towards the far corner, away from the entrance, to where I'd parked up the previous morning. Then fished out my wallet to find the exit ticket. The ticket was there, but the car had gone.

“You sure you left it here?”

“Absolutely. The place was nearly full, and I had to park it over by the fence.”

“Better ask at the gate. Maybe its been towed away? ”

Two hours later it was confirmed, my car was another entry on a long list of cars reported stolen that month. From the car park we’d gone to the police station, sat around for almost forty minutes, then spent another fifteen minutes filling in report forms. The desk sergeant’s attitude wasn’t exactly encouraging.

“They either turn up within a couple of hours, kids joyriding mostly, or disappear completely. What was it…?” he paused to check the details “Three year old Rover? Not high on the list of desirables. Probably kids. Probably turn up, Though it might be a wreck…”

He assured me that if the car showed up anywhere they’d call me. But agreed that if I didn’t hear by this time tomorrow, I might as well pick a copy of the local Auto Trader and start looking for something else. His parting shot was that I ought to consider a good alarm system.

16
Joyriding

Pouring another brandy and listening to Buddy Guy's *Damn Right, I Got The Blues* I pondered the options. Had I been the innocent victim of a bunch of bored teenagers whose ideas of fun was thrashing the nuts off a stolen car? Or was it another 'let's annoy the fucker' move by Tel and his muscle? Tel was away, but that didn't mean that much; he'd seemed surprised when I was hammered at Silverstone, so maybe that pair of gorillas were working on their own initiative? Or was it just joyriders? Some bleeding joy...

The plod rang the next day.

"We've found your car, sir."

"Great, where is it? Can I come and get it?"

"Only if you've got a trailer, sir..."

It turned out that they'd found it early that morning on an industrial estate in Botley. The patrol had been attracted to it by a warm and cosy-sounding orange glow, as the last of the fuel burned away. This sparked off three events; a call to my insurance brokers for a claim form, a call to the bank to check the balance of my deposit account, and opening up the new copy of Auto Trader. By the end of the week I was the proud owner of a blood red Alfa Romeo 156. An early one but the right one, the one with a V6 under the bonnet. I'd already decided to dig into the fund set aside for the tax bill due at the end of the month. Hopefully the insurance claim would be settled in time. If not, tough.

Meanwhile, Lianne had rung on Tuesday, to see if I fancied meeting her the next day in London.

"I'm stuck here, really, got no car..."

"Do you want me to come and get you?"

"No, don't worry, I'll get the train down."

So I took a cab up to the station. On my way back home from Oxford, from going into the police station to sign away all rights to the Rover, I'd picked up another overnight bag. This was to replace the one that had gone up in smoke with the rest of the Rover. And a new toothbrush and comb to go in it. I had this over my shoulder as I bought my train ticket.

The bag had been had been the only thing of value in the car apart from a few CDs, and the little slags who'd stolen the car had probably had it away with them anyway.

"We're reviewing the case to date, need to put a report in to our superiors. They're being leaned on by Interpol and our Dutch colleagues. I don't suppose you could get down here on Monday?"

"Yeah, no problem. But why me?"

"Appreciate your input. And my superiors want to meet you."

Nigel Sutherland's call had come when I was on the train back up to Oxford after my latest assignation with Lianne at the Halkin. Most of the rest of that Thursday was wasted playing my guitar, volume cranked up high on the pair of headphones that Hilda and Alf had bought me for Christmas. By teatime I was doing a pretty good impression of BB King. All I needed was a loud waistcoat, five more stone in weight and ten times my existing playing abilities. Oh, and to work on my tan.

I wondered what I was in for as I parked up the Alfa and pressed the alarm in the safety of an anonymous concrete office block's car park just south of Blackfriar's Bridge. Sutherland came through to get me as I was in the reception area, clipping my Visitor badge onto the lapel of my jacket.

"You found us allright, then?"

"Yes thanks, directions were fine–"

"Follow me." He nodded to the uniformed commissionaire who'd taken my details down, and walked across the staircase. "Only one floor. Quicker than taking the lift."

We walked along a glass-partitioned corridor through the centre of the building, and into a room with a red light outside. Inside was a long conference table at which were sat three people. I was introduced to them, and pointed towards a chair. Mrs Davies, a lumpy woman in her late forties, dressed in a navy suit and with close-cropped dark hair, took immediate command. She was already in the conference room when we got there; Sutherland had introduced me to her as soon as we entered the room. She directed me to a chair.

Something about her reminded me of that living legend of the racing world, Jackie Stewart. It was the hawk-like way that her clear blue-grey eyes darted around the room as she spoke.

"We're grateful for your help. It goes without saying that this is all covered by the official secrets act."

"Of course."

A real bundle of fun. Laugh-a-minute type. Along the wall behind her were pinned maps of Europe and southern England, surrounded by photographs. Pieces of red string criss-crossed the map, joining up cities and the mugshots. I recognised a couple of the photographs instantly; one was Tel Martin, familiar because it was one of the shots I'd taken what seemed like a lifetime ago in Scotland. The other I knew was of the two blokes, identical to the copy I'd put into the safe hands of Paul, who at that moment was probably in his office just across the north side of the river. Before I could take in the other images she stood up, pulled the cords of the blind, and plunged the room into twilight. A projector burst into life, and in the next half hour I was treated to a full slide show of all the suspects. One of the images was a grainy shot of my car in the truck stop at Torhout. Sutherland and I exchanged smirks as that one flashed through.

Eventually she reopened the blind and sat down. "These two are still a mystery to us." Mrs Davies pointed to the grainy shot on the wall. We know they're working for Martin, but can't trace them. They don't seem to have any record anywhere."

"I've got part of a Range Rover registration number that might connect with them." As I said this I flicked through the notepad I'd taken out of my pocket. "I thought I'd given it to you." I scribbled down the details and slipped them across the table.

"Where did this come from?" she asked me this as she dispatched one of the others, a quiet female in her early twenties who had said nothing, out of the meeting room with the piece of paper. Presumably to check the database.

"I think it was the one that was used when somebody took a look over my home."

"Did we know about this?"

Nigel Sutherland looked straight at her. "It was in the reports, ma'am. Somebody should have checked it."

"Of course." She turned back to me. "But I thought you didn't know anything beyond it being a dark-coloured Range–"

"I don't. But had a feeling it might be connected."

She shot me a look that could break granite at fifty yards. "We'll see."

Two minutes later the minion came back into the room, and passed the slip of paper to Mrs Davies, who turned to me and explained that "It's almost certainly a vehicle registered to Marsport Industries. Where did you find the number out?"

'Er, I saw it parked up at Marsport's premises."

This time her look would have shattered a five tonne block of Kryptonite in the next county. But she let it ride. In the next five minutes she summarised that the key to unlocking everything was finding out who the two men in the photograph were. Sutherland guided me back down to reception, and I was signed out again. As I handed the pass back he asked if I had time for a bite of lunch.

"Yes, nothing else planned. Can I leave my car here?"

"Sure. We can walk to the pub, it's only two minutes away."

Within five minutes I was holding a pint of Director's Bitter and looking through the Anchor's lunchtime menu.

"Her nickname's Lara. Like Lara Croft. She's a hard case. Not known for taking prisoners." We sat in the pub's dining room, overlooking the terrace that at another time of year would be an inviting place to sit. But not on a flat and cold February day when the thin fog hadn't cleared and it had barely seemed to get light. "But she's very thorough. That's how she's got to the rank she has."

"She didn't seem impressed that the Range Rover led back to Tel Martin."

"No, that's just the impression she gives. Doesn't like to be thought of as out of touch. She's pretty ruthless. It's another little bit of evidence. And it all adds up. See you've changed your car, too. Any reason? Getting bothered about people knowing it?"

"How'd you know that? Do you keep tabs on everybody?"

"Don't get paranoid... I was at the water machine when you pulled into the car park. Saw you getting out of a new car..."

As we ate lunch I switched my mobile back on. It rang a minute later with a string of messages. Two from editors wanting to talk through ideas I'd put forward at the beginning of the week during my enforced stay in the caravan. One from my mother suggesting that she might come up to stay so that she could see Hilda, and one from Lianne. They'd all keep until later.

"So why am I in the loop? I didn't think I added anything to what you already knew..."

"Despite appearances, she's grateful for your help. She knew it was part of the deal when you came on board and she's honouring it. Any news of Martin? He still seems to be out of circulation."

"No, the last I heard he was still away. No idea where–"

"Unless he slipped out through the back door, he's still in the country somewhere. You will keep us informed if he turns up, won't you?"

"Of course. And likewise?"

"Naturally."

We finished our lunch by a little after two, and I was escorted back to my car. As I crawled through the traffic along York Road, I noticed the navy blue Mondeo that had cut across a couple of cars to tuck in just behind me. It was behind me a few minutes later when I worked my way over Westminster Bridge, and still with me as I worked my way around Parliament Square and out onto Victoria Street. As I ran up Grosvenor Place towards Hyde Park Corner it was still on my tail. I reached across and found my mobile when I stopped at the lights, and pressed Sutherland's number just as they turned green. I was already halfway along Park Lane when he answered.

"Are you having me followed?"

"What?"

"I seem to be being followed by a dark blue Mondeo. Is it anything to do with you?"

"No. Why on earth should we be following you?"

"Thought not. Right, thanks, I'll deal with it."

Instead of following my original plan of carrying on heading north up Edgware Road I suddenly veered off to the left at Marble Arch and onto Bayswater Road. A cab blasted his horn as I cut across in front of him. Fuck him, I thought, I've been carved up often enough by black cabs in the West End...

This was enough to get rid of the Mondeo, who'd been right on my tail, close enough to read the number on the boot lock of the Alfa. I carried on right through past Lancaster Gate, and turned right into Queensway. Just as I'd cleared the junction at the end of the one way part of the road, I glanced in my rear view mirror and realised that the Mondeo was back, three cars behind me.

I shot a just-changing-to-red light at the top of Queensway, and two minutes later was on the slip road up to the A40. By the time I got to Hanger Lane the Mondeo was back, sitting a few cars behind me. It stayed in touch with me as I got onto the M40. I kept racking my brains, trying to remember all the tricks I'd been shown a few years earlier, when I'd been done a feature on an anti-terrorism driving course for a magazine. As I approached the Stokenchurch turn-off, where the motorway comes down to two lanes, I knew what I had to do; I ran in the middle lane at about eighty, then at the last instance blasted past a truck and cut straight across the hatched lane dividers into the slip lane. The truck driver blasted his horn. Fuck him. I watched with satisfaction as the Mondeo was given no option but to drive past, staying on the motorway. Then I slipped down to the junction and back onto the motorway; I reckoned I'd get back on a couple of hundred yards behind the two blokes in the Mondeo. I took a chance that they'd be more interested in looking ahead than behind.

My mobile rang as I slipped back into lane two.

"Hi, it's Nigel Sutherland. Got rid of your company?"

"Sort of. I'm behind them."

"Sounds like a neat trick. Can you see the index number of their car?"

"Should be able to in two minutes. I'll have to catch them up. hold on..."

I caught them up, got close enough to read the registration plate, then dropped back behind the Tesco truck I'd just passed. If I pulled a couple of yards to the offside I could still see the Mondeo, running in the middle lane. I gave the number to Sutherland and rang off. He rang again two minutes later.

"Hire car. Hertz at Heathrow rented it yesterday to Marsport. Driver's name is Bostock."

"Cheers. I owe you one. Speak to you later."

They were still ahead of me at Junction Six, and stayed on the motorway. They probably knew my address already. Not that much of a surprise, really; it was on my business cards, in the phone book, in any of the half-dozen directories of journalists. Figuring that they'd probably stay on the motorway until Junction Eight, I came off at Seven and went the scenic route to home, through Wallingford and on the back lanes towards Bennett's Farm. Instead of going straight into the drive I went past the farm entrance and reversed the car into the grass-covered lane on the other side of the road, the one leading into the woods. Then I waited.

Sure enough, about five minutes after I'd parked up a blue Mondeo drove slowly past me, the two blokes in it both looking in the opposite direction to me, looking across the lane towards my Caravan. It came back again a couple of minutes later, at a much higher speed.

I rang Sutherland again. "Just got home. They definitely know where I live."

"For God's sake be careful. You want me to have a word with your friend Granville? He could probably arrange someone to keep an eye on the place–"

"No, I should be allright, thanks. But thanks anyway."

Quarter past two. Lying in bed unable to sleep. I'd just glanced across at the clock, its digital display casting the faintest of green lights around the room. In the absolute stillness all I could hear was my own breathing, and a distant hum from the fridge. Then I heard a crunch. Not loud, but near. The crunch of a boot on frosted grass. I'd been out the last time that I'd had nocturnal visitors. This time I might meet them face to face.

I slipped out of bed and pulled on the robe that I'd dumped alongside the bed an hour earlier. The police would have gone ballistic if they realised I hadn't put the twelve bore away in its cupboard when I'd come back at dusk from a foray into the woods. After the saga with the Mondeo I'd needed to get some clear air in my head, and taking the gun out seemed a good way to do that.

I crept through the open bedroom door and into the lounge, using the pilot lights of the stereo and television as guidance. I found the edge of the table and worked around, sitting on the bench. Put my hand down onto the floor and found the cold metal. Left it and moved a few inches further away to where the cartridge belt lay. Slid a pair of cartridges out of the webbing, and swapped hands, so that they were in my left as I traced back across the floor back to where the gun lay. I lifted it carefully onto the table top, eased the lever silently to the side and felt the barrels hinge open. Slipped the shells into the waiting chambers, and heard the gun click closed with what sounded like a deafening clank. I balanced the understock against the table edge, the index finger of my right hand resting gently against the trigger. With my left hand I found the head of the Anglepoise lamp, and twisted it towards the doorway. A finger rested on the push-button, ready.

Then I waited.

I cursed the fact that all the blinds were closed. The total darkness meant I couldn't tell who was where. I Sat facing the door waiting for something to happen. It seemed like forever. Eventually the sound of the handle being tried reverberated through my head, followed by a scraping sound. A credit card moving the Yale's tang out of its slot in the frame? The door opened and I flicked on the light.

He froze, staring down the wrong end of both barrels, then turned and ran. I followed him out, and fired a single shot into the darkness, into the air. A momentary shower of red and yellow flashes emerged from the far end of the gun. A car door slammed and the roar of an engine maybe a hundred yards away. Eventually red tail lights came on, disappearing down the lane.

"What the fuck was that?" Alf shouted as he tore across the yard, gun in hand.

"Visitors. Burglars, I think. Just glad I hadn't put the–"

"You were the one who bollocked me for taking a pot-shot–"

"Yeah, but that was different..." My head was pounding, seeing red flashes. My stomach churned. My hands were shaking, twitching as the adrenaline pumped through my system. At that moment I'd a pretty good idea what colour adrenaline was. Alf eventually left, and I closed the door behind him. Turned the key in the second lock. Switched off the lights and headed back to bed. I slept fitfully for the rest of the night.

"They came back last night. One of them actually came to the door."

"Eh?"

"It was the smaller one."

"You're quite sure?"

"Saw the scar on his forehead."

"So what do you think they were after?"

"Your guess is as good as mine. I'm more concerned with why–"

"Martin's still AWoL, you know..."

I'd rung Sutherland first thing in the morning. We decided that they thought I was out again. I'd taken to parking the Alfa further into the yard, alongside Hilda's Land Rover. So that it was given a bit more protection from the floodlights on the side of their house. They would come on if anyone went near it at night. Far enough away from the caravan to look as though nobody was home. I was just wrapping up the call when Alf came to the door.

I told Hilda that you thought it was ordinary burglars."

"I'd been wondering what you'd say."

"Don't want her getting wound up about anything. Baby's due in three months–"

"And you don't want any more stress than she's already got?"

"Exactly."

We left it that so far as Hilda was concerned, my visitors had been opportunists, thinking the place was empty. And that I'd go into Oxford and get a couple of floodlights of my own, lights that would come on if anyone came near the caravan.

17

Nothing happens in February

I wasn't looking forward to it. February is the most depressing month of my year. Nothing happens. The sportscar racing is still two months away, and there's still a month to go before the start of the Formula One season.

The damp constantly wins the battle against my calor gas heating. Alf's fields are flat and grey, the woods stay shrouded in mist. Either that, or it rains. The sun never seems to come out, and I want to disappear, to hibernate. So when Neville rang me from Williams F1 and said that the interview I'd been trying to arrange with their new Brazilian hot-shot test driver, was on... But to get it would mean them flying me out to Jerez... And that I'd have to endure two nights and three days out there, it took nanoseconds to decide.

Just as I was packing, Janice rang me. "Hi Babe, any chance of getting together? I need to talk with you."

"I'm about to head off to Spain for a couple of days. Back by the weekend. Can it keep?"

"Well... wanted to tell you face to face, but... I'm leaving England for a while."

"So who's the lucky bloke?"

"You, I think. Get me off your back for a bit. No, I'm going working in Oz for a stint, at least six months. In a proper revue, too, keep my kit on for a change."

"I'm really pleased for you. All come up a bit quickly, hasn't it? So when do you go?"

"Saturday. Midday flight. Rehearsals don't start for a fortnight, but I'm going via Malaysia, have a break in the sun, work on my tan in Langkawi then on to Sydney."

"Lucky Sydney. And lucky Langkawi, too."

I finished up by wishing her well, and meant it. As I rang off I couldn't help but think that an era had come to an end. It had never been a meaningful relationship for either of us, but we'd had a lot of laughs together. It was unlikely that we'd carry on where we left off when she got back. If she ever came back. I'd miss her.

Stepping off the plane into the warmth of southern Spain was all it took to improve my state of mind. Within an hour of getting through immigration I was in the pitlane at the circuit, enjoying the bark of a temperamental qualifying engine. The last shakedown runs before the cars would be loaded into their aluminium crates, stuffed into the belly of an enormous Antonov and flown off for the first round of the season in Australia. Not this car, of course; this one was just a donkey, a development tool used to evaluate new bits. But the data fed back from this session gets integrated into the quartet of new, real, race cars under construction at Grove under the watchful eyes of a troupe of nervous and apprehensive team managers and their even more apprehensive senior engineers. Two race cars and two spares, and the first of a batch of maybe twenty race cars that will be used up, ripped up, torn apart and recycled during the course of the season.

I spent two complete evenings with Guiseppe Rivaldi, getting the story of his life in halting English. We sat around in the corner of our hotel lobby, surrounded by cool marble and warm lights, soft guitar music playing discreetly in the background. Nev helped me overcome Gio's lack of fluency; three weeks spent in his company had helped him understand Gio, and between the pair of us we got plenty for me to work with. I learned how his rôle testing new parts was part of a master plan that would hopefully see him taking a seat in the race car as soon as a vacancy occurred. Better still, I was the first hack to talk to him at length, to gain his confidence. To get his mobile number. Which might make getting hold of him easier once he hits the big time. That sort of connection has always been valuable.

"He seems a good guy."

"Yeah, he's getting on really well, popular with his engineers, too–"

"Even though he keeps breaking the car? Or are your gearbox people chipping into his salary?"

Nev and I stood watching the car being brought back on a transporter for the third time in two days.

"That's what the sessions about. We're trying different transmission combinations–"

"You might find one that works by the time you get to Monza..."

He threw a gentle, exaggerated cartoon punch at my chest, then strolled off towards the garage. I leaned on the pitlane wall for a couple of minutes, then decided to go and have a cigarette in the lee of the team motorhome.

Three of the other English-based Grand Prix teams were at Jerez, and all four were jealously guarding their territories. This didn't stop me from picking up a few snippets to go along with the main story I'd gone to get. By the time I landed back in England I was feeling pretty positive about life. Then Nigel Sutherland screwed it all up nicely.

18

Head, hands and feet

Half a mile from home. Flicking the 156 through the bends after clearing Wheatley, enjoying the buzz of power and a sharp chassis. I fumbled in my pocket and retrieved my phone, pressing the answer button in Braille.

"Where have you been? We've been trying to reach you."

"Spain. Test session."

"I'd appreciate you letting me know when you are leaving the country–"

"I spend half my working life out of the country. Anyway–"

"Essex police have found a corpse. A few days ago. In a disused quarry between Colchester and Witham."

"What's it got to do with me?"

"Headless. Hands had been cut off, too."

"And...?"

"They found the head a day later, in a sack off a lay-by on the A127."

"Good for them, But what's it got to do with me?"

"It was Tel Martin."

I pulled over into the entranceway of a field. I was stunned. Sutherland must have expected me to be. He said nothing for a lifetime that probably lasted fifteen seconds.

"Thought you'd be surprised."

"More than surprised. I'm staggered. I presume they've no idea of who or why?"

"Why doesn't call for Einstein to work out. And how was pretty easy once they'd found the head. Too. There was a bullet hole in the front of the skull. Right between the eyes. And they found a nine millimetre slug in the back of the brain."

I took another few seconds to digest what he was telling me. Then asked him "But no idea who?"

"You better meet me. Uxbridge? Soon as you can?"

I glanced at my watch. An hour to get there. "Tonight? I can be there for about nine thirty."

My first thought was to call Lianne. But then I thought again. Was I supposed to know about Tel's demise? Something told me I'd better wait until the news started to filter through from other sources. I turned around and started to drive down to meet Sutherland. Halfway down the M40 my mobile rang.

"It's Lianne. I need to see you. Can you come over here?"

So she knew. But then she probably would by now. She'd probably had to identify the remains. "I'm on my way back from up North" I thought quickly, working a way out to explain why I'd need to allow for the detour. "And can get straight to you. But it might be nearly midnight." Keep up the pretence. "Won't Tel be around, though?" 'I'm going to dump him.' I could recall the way she'd said it.

"No, he won't be around." She sounded flat, terminally subdued. Like I hoped she would.

Sutherland was already sat in the bar, in a corner of the surprisingly quiet lounge. This bit of Uxbridge didn't seem get much of whatever nightlife action the town might have. He asked what I'd like to drink, then pushed a large flat envelope across the table and stood up. By the time he'd come back from the bar I'd studied all three photographs. One of a naked, decapitated and handless torso lying on a steel table. And two of the head that went with it, a profile shot and one head-on. Hard light, lit from all around, no shadows. The torso had been washed, had a waxy sheen, and the head was spotlessly clean, too. Eyes closed, face set in a strangely peaceful expression. A neat, round, dark hole was where the bridge of his nose would have been. The hair was swept back, flattened against the skull. I looked at the back from the profile shot, but couldn't tell what damage there was.

"Not pretty, is it?" He placed the half of bitter on a beermat and sat down.

"No, but it's definitely Tel."

"Still haven't found the hands."

"Why'd they dismembered him anyway?"

"Delay the time it took to identify him, probably. And if a bloke taking his dog for a walk hadn't come across the binsack with the head in it, it might have worked. No tattoos, no scars, so it could have been heaven-knows-how-long before anyone knew whose body it was."

"But the torso's definitely Tel's?"

"Certainly. The forensic people did a match. Apparently even the hack marks match."

I felt myself grimace. We paused for a moment, then a couple came towards the next table so he slipped the ten-eight prints back into their envelope. "What we need to know is where he's been for the past couple of weeks. They reckon he was found – or at least the body was – within a day or two of being killed."

We finished our drinks and walked out into the car park, assuring each other that we'd keep in touch. I got into the car, fished out Dylan's greatest hits, and slotted it onto the player. Then guided the nose of the Alfa back towards the M25, and Epping. The answer, my friend, is blowing in the wind. It's bloody somewhere.

"Oh Mark, thanks for coming. I've been desperate to see you. Been trying to get you all night..." Her eyes were ringed red. And it was the first time I'd seen her with barely any make-up and not dripping with gold. She was wearing a simple black dress, her long hair piled high on her head and pinned into place with what looked like a black bow-tie.

"Sorry, been in Spain with Williams and then straight up to a meeting on the other side of Birmingham."

"Anyway, you're here now..."

"Yeah, so what's happened?"

"It's Terry... he's... dead."

"What!?" I mustered the most surprised and horrified expression I could manage. Oscar-winning stuff. Or at least a Bafta.

"Murdered. The police have been here all afternoon, then I had to go with them and..."

I mixed her a vodka and tonic, and made one for myself. Then sat next to her on the chesterfield sofa and listened while she told me how the events of the day had unfolded. How she'd got back from a trip to the supermarket to find a police car sitting outside the locked gates, waiting for her. How a uniformed policewoman told her that a body had been found almost a week earlier, but that they had only just been able to put him "into a condition where he might be identified".

How they'd asked he to go with them to the mortuary, pulled back a sheet, and she'd seen, and recognised, her husband. She sobbed for breath once, momentarily. Then excused herself, blew her nose on a tissue, and carried on, draining her glass and waving it towards me for a refill. "It was terrible, Mark. They'd only pulled the cover back to his chin, but there was a hole right between his eyes."

I stopped the words 'I know' before they even started to form in my throat. Eventually she sat silently, watching the flames of the imitation log fire in the inglenook opposite. From what she said, they'd reunited the components before showing her the corpse. I'd once heard that they use a length of brush stave when they have to reconnect a severed head. I wondered if it was true as I looked across at Lianne. "So who's likely to have–"

"Don't be naïve, Mark. You know Terry. He's more enemies than friends. Had."

I grunted in agreement. We sat for another half hour, talking about the stress of her day. Then she declared she was hungry, that she hadn't eaten since breakfast. We went through to the kitchen and she started to make a sandwich.

"I've not even put my car away. Would you mind..."

"Not at all."

She tossed me the keys, and told me that the fourth button on the fob would open the garage door. I went out, got into the Mercedes, and fired it up. The door, the first of three, the one nearest the porch of the house, slid upwards and a light came on in the garage. I pulled the car inside. Tel's Jaguar was in the next bay.

We spent the night together, in the marital bed. But we didn't screw; she'd taken a tranquilliser and slept like she was in a coma. My night was fitful, images of Tel's severed head mixing in with older ones of Mike Lewis and a bloke with the expression of a startled rabbit staring down the barrels of my shotgun. Somebody sawing a length off a brush handle.

I was already sat downstairs in the kitchen drinking a coffee when she appeared. "Can I pour you one?"

"Thanks, darlink, I'd really appreciate one. Thanks for staying with me..."

Driving home an hour later, having assured Lianne that I'd be on the other end of my mobile all weekend and until at least the middle of the week, I felt more than a little confused. So who'd killed Tel? And why?

I rang Nigel Sutherland.

"Did you know that Martin didn't use his car on his last journey?"

"Does he just have the one?"

"So far as I know–"

"Chap in his position, surely he'd be able to get his hands on something else to drive?"

"Has anyone spoken to the female he went to the Channel Islands with yet?"

My weekend plans of doing nothing had been neatly twisted into knots by what had happened since I got off the Williams charter aircraft at Birmingham International. Which was why I was sat in front of my laptop when I should have been in the pub, trying to write up news items from Jerez. The phone was jammed between my chin and shoulder.

“I believe our colleagues from SCS are with her.”

“Will you let me know if anything–”

“Of course. Like I said, you’re in the loop. How did you know about Martin’s car, anyway?”

“Let’s just say I have my sources.” No point in letting him know that I’d spent the night with Lianne. “Is anyone keeping watch on Paul Stevenson?”

“Of course.”

Of course. He rang off, promising to keep me appraised of any developments.

The news stuff was finished off, and dispatched by e-mail so that it would be ready to drop into the magazines that would be in newsagents by the middle of the week. Then to the fridge for a beer. Finding none there I pulled on a heavy coat and boots and walked to the Marquis for a pint instead. *‘I’m going to dump him.’* Had she? I sank four pints of Old Hooky, chatted with Mikey about nothing, and shoved the concept to the back of my mind.

I was with Lianne when Sutherland rang me on Tuesday afternoon. I told him I’d call him back later, and went back to where we’d been sitting together on her sofa.

“Anything important?”

“Nothing that won’t keep until later. An editor wanting to talk through an idea.”

“Anyway, the police. They’ve been here twice over the weekend and again this morning. They went through Terry’s office, took it apart, left it in a mess. Went off with boxes full of stuff…”

“They any clues who?”

“Not that they are telling me…”

We lapsed back into silence. I leaned forward and poured her another glass of wine. “Have you eaten?”

“Not since last night. I haven’t much appetite…”

“You ought to eat something.” Jesus, I was lapsing into stuff from the Boy’s Own Book of Pointless Platitudes for the Bereaved.

“I was going to the village earlier for some bread, but then the police arrived again–”

“Would you like me to go and get some? Will the store still be open?”

I used the time it took to drive into the village to call Nigel Sutherland back. “Sorry about that. It was a bit tricky. What’s happening?”

“We could do with you coming over to go through the latest developments. Mrs Davies asked me to call you. How soon can you get down?"

"Can it keep until morning? I'm tied up tonight, but can be with you by about ten thirty–"

"That should be fine. You sure you're not able to get down this evening?"

"Absolutely. Tomorrow, then..."

We ate almost as soon as I got back with the bread, washing down corned beef sandwiches with a bottle of a light red from Provence. That night we screwed. Hard. It was as though she was making up for the night of abstinence after she'd identified Tel's body.

Sutherland again came down to collect me from the reception desk, and led me straight into the conference room. There was a new picture on the wall. Another one of Tel, life size and face on, this one with his eyes open. Open but flat, dull, very lifeless. And separated by the small dark hole on the bridge of his nose. 'Lara' Davies came bustling into the room as I was studying this post mortem portrait.

"So, who do you think did it?"

"He didn't have a butler..."

She shot me one of her laser looks. Then went over to the table, sat herself down, and opened the folder she'd carried into the room. "From what we can gather he had more enemies than friends..." she was interrupted by the door opening. A large man came through the portal, turning slightly sidewards to ease his way. Short cropped hair, a well cut double breasted navy suit, and a white shirt providing a stark contrast against the blackness of his skin. He nodded to the other occupants of the room, but made a beeline for me.

"Peter Lawrence, Scotland Yard. You must be Mr McDermott." He extended his hand, shook mine. As I nodded to confirm who I was, I nursed a set of knuckles that felt like they'd never function again after their crushing. He was followed into the room by a much smaller man with polecat features, a face full of angles and a puny body wrapped in a cheap suit that hung shapelessly from his bony shoulders. He was introduced as Detective Sergeant Scase. Then a tray of coffee arrived, its bearer pouring everybody in the room a cup before taking her leave.

Eventually everybody settled and Mrs Davies stood, then spoke. "Right, This has devolved into an unholy mess. Our prime suspect has been bumped off, but at least van Drel is still in custody in Maastricht. Are we any nearer identifying the two heavies that have been causing such inconvenience?"

"They're being followed. They've been identified as William 'Billy' Henderson, that's him on the left..." Lawrence pointed towards the pinned up photograph on the wall behind him "... and George Bostock Known as G. Neither have got form, but they've been attracting interest from the drug squad for some time."

I sat and looked at the large policeman, then spoke. "So do you think it could have been the Dutch connection that killed Tel Martin?"

"Possibly. We're liaising with the local force, and from what we can gather they weren't happy that Martin's men went blundering in after they'd found out we'd switched the merchandise." The polecat-featured man spoke in a voice as thin as his nose.

"So have they sent somebody over here?" Mrs Davies seemed keen to get back in control of the meeting's agenda.

"We aren't sure. Nobody's been able to make a direct connection. But it looks likely." Polecat face fixed me with clear blue eyes.

I asked the obvious question, obvious to me at least. "Why Martin? Why not Stevenson? And are the Dutch taking it all seriously?"

"Don't know why–"

Polecat was interrupted by Lawrence. "We're keeping the pressure up. And we have somebody watching Stevenson and the other two. We'll just have to see what turns up. So far as I'm concerned Martin's no great loss to the world..."

The conversation went round in circles for a while, but I came out of the meeting with the clear impression that nobody was particular grieving for Tel, and that Paul Stevenson had been elevated to the top of the pile. As I walked back towards my car, Nigel Sutherland accompanied me.

"Sorry, can't manage to do lunch today." He glanced at his watch "Anyway, it's a bit early. Do you think Stevenson's got the brains to run the operation? "

"Possible. Not likely but possible. Do you reckon he got pissed off with the way Tel Martin was treating him?"

"I can only go off what you told me, but it's possible. Something about that doesn't add up, though..."

"Which means there's somebody else running the game?"

"Could be. We'll keep you informed. Take care."

I got into my car, fired up the engine, and pushed a CD into the player. Springsteen's *Thunder Road* blasted through the speakers. Made me want to drive fast, to get away from all this hassle, to pull the wheel back and fly away to somewhere warm and stress free. Instead I filtered into the crawling morass of London, along the south bank of the river, crossing at Westminster Bridge. It took me almost two hours to get home. I left my phone switched off until I pulled into the yard and parked up alongside Hilda's Land Rover. I needed time to think. About motive, means and opportunity.

The bench behind my table was where I spent most of the afternoon. I collected my post from Hilda, but she'd been busy cooking, so was glad to exchange greetings and let me go back home. With Classic FM playing in the background I worked through what I knew, or thought I knew.

Paul Stevenson just didn't seem sharp enough to run the entire operation on his own. Not even with a couple of willing thugs fighting his battles for him. I'd first met him maybe seven years back, when he joined Marsport from one of the little Formula Ford teams. He'd always struck me as a prat. But a murderous prat? I didn't think so.

Or maybe it was the other two blokes, G and Billy, that were calling the shots. Maybe they'd got pissed off waiting for Tel, who was likely to have been cautious. Maybe they'd mistaken Tel's long view for dithering. Maybe they'd seized the initiative. The pain behind my eyes was getting worse. I dozed off to the strains of Elgar's *Cello Concerto* playing as the grey day faded to black.

19

A change is a good as arrest

My mobile rang as I walking back across the yard, flicking through the morning's post. A fistful of press releases, the phone bill and a postcard with a picture of a giant carved eagle on its front. 'Weather here, wish you were wonderful. Love, J' She'd mailed the card from Langkawi, but was probably in Sydney by the time it arrived.

I pressed the button to take the call.

"Hello Mark. We've arrested all three of them. Got them this morning. Well, DI Lawrence did. They're in custody at Paddington Green. We'll be going over this afternoon to interview them. Just thought I'd let you know."

"Thanks Nigel, so you'll let me know what comes–"

"Naturally. Don't let anybody know, for now at least."

"Of course."

Paddington Green. The place that forever seemed to get mentions in reports of terrorist cases. Supposed to be the highest security facility that the Metropolitan Police have got. They are taking these guys seriously. I finished opening the post, pinned the postcard up onto the front of the fridge with a magnet that my Mum had bought me, and flicked on the kettle.

I made my drink, then I rang Lianne. "How are you doing?"

"Allright. I've had the police here again, going through everything. Took the office apart again. They've even taken Terry's car away–"

"Didn't find anything?"

"They're not saying, even if they did. Can you meet me in London tomorrow, usual place, about one? Could do with a complete change."

"No problem. See you there."

She was already sat at a table in the window when I walked into the Bistro St Omer. A bottle of Vin de Pays already on the table, her glass half full. Looking stunning in a sharply-tailored black suit. Her legs tanned and slender from the bottom of a pencil skirt.

"You look wonderful."

"Thanks, darlink. I've had that whining bitch Diane and that idiot husband of hers around or on the phone every few hours for the past two days. Keeps talking about organising the funeral. Not that there's any point. We won't even hear until the end of the week when they will release the body..."

Her eyes were fiery. She clearly resented the intrusion from her sister-in-law. And she wasn't wearing the lettered necklace anymore. Had she worn it recently? I Couldn't remember. She took a sip from her glass, then spoke again. "Let's order."

Almost as soon as she'd uttered the words a waiter appeared and placed two menus down on the corner of the scrubbed oak table top. She ordered a warm tuna salad – no starter – and I followed her lead, ordering the same.

"She was asking about the will, too. But I told her that she needn't worry, her precious showroom is still hers, Don't want the damned place–"

"And what about Marsport? What are you going to do with that?"

"Leave it running. Paul can keep on top of it. He's off at the moment, his wife rang in and said he needed to be away for a couple of days, but everybody else can just carry on."

So she didn't know that he'd been arrested. I couldn't say anything. I wasn't supposed to know, either. So I went with the flow of her conversation. "What about sponsorship for the team? I heard that Kentucky had pulled out..."

She fixed me with a gimlet stare. Then it softened. "There should be enough to run at least part of the season. And the agency are looking for something else."

The Agency. Was this what Tel used to call his coke-smuggling operation? "The agency?"

"MDC. Those people who find sponsorship. Terry got a call from them last month... before..."

Before somebody drilled him with a nine millimetre and chopped him into little pieces. Lianne reached for her glass, this time taking a gulp not a sip.

That afternoon, instead of checking into the hotel room across the park, we drove back up to my place. We cleared the village and she turned her Mercedes into my lane. I apologised in advance for the state of the place. "I've been pretty busy, the place is a tip–"

"If I was attracted to you by your domestic skills..."

"How come you want to come back here anyway? Thought you'd be more comfortable at– "

"Diane keeps appearing. I want to put clear space between us. My mobile's already off."

She parked up at the side of the caravan, and I let us both in, going straight across to light the heater. It was almost dark, and the floodlights came on in the yard almost as I parked up. Somebody had triggered the sensor: I was about to get a visit. I introduced Hilda and Lianne to each other as soon as Hilda came through the door.

"Sorry to disturb you, but thought you ought to know straight away. The police have been round. Some bloke in a suit. Left this card, asked if you'd get in touch with him as soon as you got home." She'd already started to leave, but said 'Bye, nice to meet you..." to Lianne as she went through the door.

"Thanks Hilda, I'll get back to him..." I said, to her disappearing back.

Lianne gave me a look that told me she wasn't in the least bit surprised that the police had been looking for me. "Is that something to do with...?"

"Possibly. I'll call him later."

"You better call him now. It sounded urgent."

About the last thing I wanted was to let Lianne get so much as a sniff of the amount of information I held on Tel. Instinct told me I couldn't even hint that I knew anything beyond what I'd legitimately found out from interviewing him, and what she'd told me. As I walked over to the phone I thought fast. Punched in the number, waited for the connection. Hoped that DS Scase would get the thread of my problem. Hoped he was bright enough. His extension answered.

"Hi, My Name's McDermott. Believe you called around to see me?"

"Thanks for getting back. Appreciate it. I need your help, I'm trying to–"

I cut him short. "Tomorrow? Yes, I can get in tomorrow. What time?"

"It'll do over the phone–"

"Ten thirty? Where?"

"Oh, um, presume you can't talk–"

"Yes I know it. Paddington Green? Can I park anywhere nearby? Do I ask for you?"

It worked. I'd managed to get away without having to say anything within earshot of Lianne that would hint that I was more involved than she thought I was. While I was on the phone She stood as though she was studying the big signed print on the wall between the lounge and bedroom, the one of Mansell in his Williams that I'd got him to sign after he'd won the Championship. But I could feel that she was watching me throughout. As I put the handset back down she started quizzing me. "What are they after? Is it to do with Terry?"

"Yeah, they just want to know what background I can give them."

"Why you?"

"Don't know. Maybe because someone's told them I'm writing his biog?" She seemed satisfied. I pulled a bottle of wine out from the carrier bag. Ferreted in the drawer under the sink, found the corkscrew, and poured a couple of glasses.

"Things have moved on a bit since I called you." Scase talked as he led me through the secure doors at the front of Paddington Green police station, and opened the blue door of an interview room. "Coffee?"

"Thanks, that'd be good."

He put his head around the door and ordered up coffee for three. "I presume you would have had difficulty talking last night."

"Yes, would've been awkward. So what's been happening?"

"DI Lawrence will be here in a minute. He's just finished another round of interviews. He'll fill you in..."

Even before he had finished the door opened, and the bulk of his superior eased its way into the room. He shook my hand, and mindful of what happened last time, I tensed my own, ready. Lawrence settled himself into one of the quartet of moulded blue chairs that were arranged, in two pairs, either side of the rectangular table. The chair seemed to groan under his bulk. There was a tape recorder on a shelf alongside his elbow, but he ignored it. The coffee arrived, and as the uniformed policeman who'd brought it left, Lawrence began to unravel what he was ready to tell me.

"The two muscle, Henderson and Bostock, are saying next to nothing. Even when we showed them pictures of their activities in West London, and told them that the Dutch police had watched them getting heavy over there, they said nothing. Both singing from the same hymn sheet. Got a smart lawyer, too. But they've both been charged with a raft of offences under the Dangerous Drugs Act, which means we can keep them right out of circulation. And we can keep going over to the Scrubs and questioning them."

"I presume you've enough to make a case stick?"

"Should have, But it's Stevenson that's proving easier. Just isn't in their league."

"So what's he saying?"

"This is where it gets interesting. He's coughed to being responsible for the deal in Belgium. Your photos and the film that our colleagues over there got were enough to crack that one. Blamed Martin, says he was put into a position where he had no choice."

"But what about Martin's death? Anything to say about that?"

"That's where it gets really interesting. And that's probably also why his sphincter's twitchier than a man with a cough who's just taken a handful of laxatives... Reckons he might have been next. He blames the Dutch. But I'm not sure we've got to the bottom of it all. I reckon there's somebody else over here, that's why I asked you to come in. See if you can come up with any ideas."

I sat back and shook my head. All the way down the line I'd had it pegged as Tel Martin's operation, with G and Billy as muscle and Paul Stevenson as the gopher. Eventually, after a prompt in the form of a cough from the Stoat, who'd been quietly sitting back while Lawrence spoke, I pulled a few thoughts together. "I didn't think Stevenson would have the bottle or the brains to be running things. Tel Martin was another matter. He was sharp, ruthless, mean, and hungry for cash - and those were his good points."

"So who do you think killed Martin?"

"Somebody who had got extremely pissed off with him."

"That much we have managed to work out for ourselves." Lawrence's eyes flashed hard.

"If he's sent his blokes in to sort out the Dutch, reckoning that they'd ripped him off, he'd be setting himself up for a good hiding, or worse. What makes you think otherwise?"

"Partly what van Drel told the Dutch police. They sent me a transcript, and so far as he's concerned, the matter was eventually settled; he thought he'd convinced Martin that somebody else would have had to pull a switch of the goods. van Drel's offered to roll over, and he's named his bosses and associates. They're being picked up..." He glanced at his watch "...about now."

"But can you believe him?"

"No reason not to. Spoke with the head of the Drug Squad in Amsterdam who's running their investigation, and he seems sure it wasn't a load of lies. His take on issues is that they realised that there was a hole in the system somewhere, but they were looking longer term, and wanted to open up another pipeline using the same people."

"Which is what makes you think that somebody was pulling Tel's strings, and that they got pissed off with him for losing the merchandise?"

"Precisely."

We sat for another twenty minutes, bouncing the same concepts around. It transpired that van Drel was working for a local chapter of

Hell's Angels. I learned that the Angels had been heavily into the drug scene for almost as long as they'd been in existence. "Like the Masons, only more paranoid. more secretive" was how Lawrence described them to me. For years they'd been able to function through their own fraternities in different countries, but there'd been some problems with the English chapters, who'd been more or less blown apart because they'd been falling out with rival gangs of outlaw bikers.

"Some of the main movers are dead and others are in prison" he explained "and so they'd had to find another route, another way of shifting their stuff around Europe. Oh, and it turns out that Stevenson was a wannabe biker in his youth, and had a couple of mates that were in the Hell's Angels–"

"So it was just a matter of tying them up with Tel Martin?"

"Something like that. You know he's got a Death's Head tattoo on his right shoulder blade? Thing is, though, there's still a gap, it doesn't quite string together. We'll keep chiselling away at Stevenson, but..."

I finally came around to his way of thinking. It was left that I'd see if I could think of anybody who could have been another layer of management over the late, but not much missed, Tel Martin. And I couldn't take the concept of Paul Stevenson as a dirty, greasy outlaw biker seriously. He gave me the impression of being too soft to handle a Peugeot 50cc scooter. The idea of him on a monster Harley-Davidson was just beyond the bounds of my imagination.

Five minutes after being escorted to the front door of the station I fished Scase's card out of my pocket and rang him. "I've been fucking clamped." The meter I'd parked on, in Hall Lane just behind the station, had run out and there was a bright yellow piece of metal around the offside front wheel. And a damned big sticker across the middle of the screen warning me not to attempt moving the vehicle. It took almost forty minutes, but at least Scase managed to pull rank and get me mobile again. Without my having to pay the fixed penalty.

I called Nigel Sutherland as soon as I got on the M40. "Just come away from Paddington Green. They seem close to putting them away."

"Yes, but... There's still the matter of who's ultimately pulling the strings."

"What about Tel's girlfriend?"

"We've checked her out. Seems pretty self-contained, though. Name's Shirley McLane–"

"Not the–?"

He snorted a laugh. "No, another one. Different spelling. She's got a florist's in Kilburn. Lives in a flat over the shop. Nice place. Never makes waves. Not so much as an unpaid parking ticket. According to Essex police, who sent someone over there when we told them about her, she was distraught when they informed her Martin had been killed. Either she's a brilliant actress–"

"Shirley McLean is..."

"– or it was for real."

"And you think it was genuine."

"Quite."

Back home I cranked up the heater, made a half-hearted gesture at clearing up, and put the kettle on for a drink. Then stretched out on the bench and went through the events of the past couple of weeks. Even went as far as getting a pad and sketching out a sort of flowchart that linked together the players. A phone call from Chris at Auto Racing yanked me back into the real world.

"Hi Mark, got a problem, was promised a piece on Gerhard Berger, been let down. Can you knock one out for me? Background, plus where he's going with BMW. Need it by close of play tonight..."

So that was the rest of the day taken care of. And enough of a distraction to stop me having to think about winners and losers, of dead bodies and Hell's Angels and gas bottles of Class A drugs.

20
Singing canaries

Lianne's call came as I was shutting down my laptop late that evening. "Can you get away for a few days? I was thinking of going over to our place in Tenerife and don't want to go on my own."

"When?"

"Day after tomorrow, Come back next Monday or Tuesday."

"Should be able to. Got a few things to sort out, but I can get those done tomorrow."

"Wonderful, darlink. I'll sort the tickets, ring you tomorrow with details."

I sat back, then grabbed my pad and scribbled down the things I needed to sort out. Call Nev and see if his offer of a free ride out to Melbourne for the season opener next month was still on. Tell Nigel Sutherland I would be away for a few days, and get him to let everyone else know. See if Hilda'd run me down to Heathrow as soon as I know when I'm flying. She couldn't; I'd have to pay for long-stay parking. Dig out some Chinos and T-shirts.

Sitting in the front end of the Iberia jet, sipping a complimentary glass of Cava as the plane levelled out and we hit cruising altitude.

"Couldn't bear to be in the back, with those terrible cramped seats. Or worse still on a bloody charter."

"Know what you mean. I get a bit spoiled. Most of the teams fly me around Club, it's a culture shock when I have to join the rabble. When I'm paying my own way its different, of course, but that doesn't happen very often–"

"Can't remember the last time I travelled anything other than Club..."

Within a couple of hours we touched down at Madrid, and were swept straight through to our connection out to the Canaries. It took longer, but at least it was longer with elbow room. By three we were stood in the warmth of a Canarian afternoon, waiting for our baggage to amble out of the hatch and onto the carousel. Through immigration, my bag over my shoulder and pulling Lianne's Samsonite behind me, I followed her as she strode towards the taxi rank. But she didn't stop there. She carried on across the main service road, towards the long term car park. Put her head into the cabin, said something in Spanish to the guy sitting there, peeled off and handed him a few notes from a roll she fished out of her handbag, and was handed a set of keys. Then she nodded to me to carry on following her.

"This yours?"

"Yes, darlink. Keep it here. Easier than using taxis."

I watched her ease the bright yellow SLK through the network of roads around the airport and out, following the signs towards Las Americas. She'd already pressed the button to drop the roof, and her case and my bag were in the shallow space behind the seats where I'd been directed to put them.

"So, how long you had a place out here?" I paused for her reply while she pushed buttons on the stereo, finally finding the English language station relayed from mainland Spain.

"About ten years. I like the climate, especially during the winter. God, I hate winters at home, so wet and cold–"

"How often do you come out?"

"Try and get here about every six weeks." She tapped her fingers in rhythm with Santana's *Samba Pa Ti* that was punctuating the commercials for Irish pubs and bars selling English roast dinners.

She turned off the main highway at the first sign for Los Cristianos. I could see the ocean glimmering beyond the orange rooftops of the apartment blocks. She carried on down the hill, turning left just before it curved around to the town centre.

"There's a remote in the glove box. Would you get it for me?"

I passed her the little black box, which she dropped into her lap. Second later she picked it up again and pressed the red button. As we turned into the gap in a ten-feet high white wall with terracotta tiles along its top, the gates were already swinging open.

"Wow, this is some place." I'd expected to be taken to one of the thousands of apartments that we'd driven past on our way through the edge of town. Not to an elegant bow-fronted villa with canopied doorway and double garage, and cascades of rich ruby red flowers covering half the front walls. She just turned towards me and smiled, then stepped out of the car and strode across to the front porch, twisting the bunch of car keys until she found the one that fitted the front door. I retrieved the luggage – hearing the gates clank shut behind me – and followed her into the cool, tiled hallway. Within an hour we were sitting, she in bikini and me in shorts, by the side of the pool. Looking over the Atlantic, with a glass of wine apiece.

Next morning Lianne declared that she'd be out for a couple of hours. "Going to the gym. You're welcome to come along… but somehow you've never struck me as a gym person."

She was dead right. I have an allergy to organised exercise. And disorganised exercise, come to that. So she drove off to her club and I settled down at the pool-side with a fresh cafétiére of coffee and my airport novel. Then I remembered something from the afternoon before. I'd been looking for a corkscrew, and following Lianne's suggestion had checked out the drawers in the dining room's wall unit. There was one in there – but there were also a couple of floppy discs. I ambled back through and opened the drawer. Took out the pair of black, unlabelled diskettes, then started to look around for the computer. There wasn't one. There might be something on them or there might not. I took a punt on her not realising that they'd disappeared and slipped the floppies into the side pocket of my weekend bag. Then went back to the pool and carried on reading the latest Ruth Rendell, the one I'd grabbed on my way through the newsagents at Heathrow.

Lianne arrived back at mid-day. Looking cool, but declaring herself hot. "Come and help me shower." That set off a pattern for three of the next four mornings – she gave herself Sunday off – and by the time it came to the last day she was looking lithe and fit, and I'd dropped into having a nap each afternoon.

We sat in a little tapas bar, eating our way through a dozen small platters of seafood and salads. I poured us another glass of Marques de Tomares Gran Reserva apiece. As I was helping myself to another portion of lightly battered squid Lianne placed her hand on mine.

"Would you mind if you go back on your own?"

"No, why?"

"That call earlier. It was from my agent here. I could do with going over a couple of things with her. I'll follow you back Wednesday."

"Agent?"

"Looks after the villa. Does the laundry and cleaning. Sorts the pool cleaner, that sort of thing. I'll take you to the airport in time…"

Twelve hours later I was taking off, heading for home. It occurred to me, after I'd battled with a bag of complimentary cashews and had the first of several drinks, that she could probably have sorted out the villa while we were both there.

There were only three messages on my mobile when I switched it back on as I settled into my seat on the bus out to the long-stay car park at Heathrow. All from Nigel Sutherland, each more urgent than the one before. As soon as I got into my car I rang him back.

"Thanks for getting back to me. Where are you?"

"Waiting for my car to warm up, sat in the middle of nowhere, near Terminal Four."

"I'm still in the office. Don't suppose you could come over here before you go home?"

I glanced at the clock; 19:43. "Could do. It'll take me a good half hour..."

"Really appreciate it."

Forty minutes later the barrier swung up and let me into the car park at Southwark. I was surprised by the number of lights still blazing in the office block. I commented on it as we walked through from the front desk towards the conference room.

"Busy place. Customs criminals are no respecters of the standard working day. We work when they do, and then go into overtime."

"So what's the urgency?"

"There've been some serious developments."

"Such as?"

"Biggest one is that Stevenson tried to top himself. Managed to slash his wrists, but they found him before it was too late. Now he's in the hospital wing at Wandsworth. And he's finally started talking."

"Saying what?"

"That he'd set the whole thing up, but that he was sidelined. By the end he was just an operative, that Tel told him how to do things. Most important, though, is that he's named the big boss..." He paused to pump me a coffee from the thermos thing on a side table "... and the late Tel. It seems, was having his strings pulled."

"Thought you'd already worked that out?"

"We had, But we didn't by who."

"By whom." He aimed a killer glance at me, then smirked.

"By whom. Bloody pedantic journalists... Anyway, we know who she is. Only thing is, we don't know where she is."

"She?" An awful, cold chill sensation suddenly made my throat go dry. I gulped at my coffee. Fortunately it was tepid.

"His lovely wife. But we've lost her."

"She's in Los Cristianos."

"How do you know that? There's no trace of her leaving the country. But she isn't at home. We went over there the other day, team-handed, but the place was locked up and her cleaning woman says she went off before the weekend and... Are you sure she's there?"

"Positive. She drove me to the airport in Tenerife at nine this morning."

"Shit."

Which is how I came to explain that I'd been screwing her since before Christmas. And how I hadn't the slightest clue that she was involved.

Sutherland took all this in, and slowly shook his head. "This means that any testimony you give is likely to be laughed out of court–"

"I wasn't to know..." I suffered deja vu. I was back in front of my Dad when I was maybe six or seven, and he'd just found out that I'd been with a couple of kids who'd nicked Mars Bars from Mrs Pickering's shop in the village. And I felt every bit as vulnerable. Lara Croft entered the room, surmising in milliseconds that something was seriously amiss. She listened, drilling occasional holes in my forehead, while this latest batch of intelligence was related to her.

"Fuck" was her initial response, followed by "Double fuck with bells on."

I was tempted to tell them that it was none of their business who I slept with, or even with whom I slept, but decided against it. I'd like to be able to leave Southwark with my balls still attached. The next ten minutes were spent relating everything I knew. About the flights, about the villa, about what she'd done and what I'd done not just in Tenerife, but in all the time I'd known Lianne. Sutherland scribbled everything down, and they both left the room. Within five minutes they were back.

"She was travelling under the name of Margarita Roberts. Hadn't you realised she was using an alias?"

"No. Everyone tended to call her Madam."

Lara blasted me with another one of her looks. Then she carried on talking, explaining that the Spanish police would get in touch with their colleagues on Tenerife and see if they could track her down. "The description you gave us where the villa is wasn't a lot of help. According to Rodriguez, their local bloke says it could be any of a few dozen places. And their land ownership registry system won't give us much to work with, either, from what Rodriguez told me. The records are pretty screwed up, thanks to the amount of, er, dubious money that has been pumped into strange timeshare property deals over the past fifteen years or so. Seems that every villain in Europe with a boxful of cash under the mattress has bought into those islands. The banks didn't used to ask a lot of questions about provenance, apparently."

As she spoke she gradually calmed down, going as far as giving me a peace offering in the form of pouring me another coffee. She even passed me the plate so I could take a chocolate biscuit. It was about nine thirty by the time she finished. I was escorted out of the building by Nigel Sutherland. He was pretty cool, but then he would be, seeing as I'd really pissed all over the work they'd been doing. I got home and pondered the idea of going to the pub, then thought better of it and drank a half bottle of brandy instead. Atilla woke me from my coma at a little before eight the next morning.

I pulled on a tracksuit, made a coffee, and emptied the dirty clothes out of my weekend bag, then toddled across the yard for the loan of Hilda's washing machine.

"So how was Spain? Looks like it was warmer than here..." She glanced out of the window at the murky mist. Then poured me a cup of tea from a pot that never seems to get cold. She eased her almost six months pregnant self onto a chair and carried on. "You haven't forgotten you Mum's coming up this weekend, have you?"

"Damn, I had. I take it she's staying..."

"Yes, don't worry. Already sorted the spare room out for her. She won't interfere with your obviously busy social life–"

"I reckon that'll be quieter for a little while–"

"Five days with one woman too much for your system to cope with? Even a classy bird like her?"

I wasn't inclined to go into too much detail. "Yeah, something like that."

"When are you off to Australia?"

"Next Thursday. Should be back the following Tuesday."

"You'll be knackered."

"Probably. But at least I should be able to get some sleep on the plane home."

Alf, Shep trailing at his heels, arrived in for a mid-morning drink, "to defrost, s'much as anything, mate." he told me. After a bit more small talk, just enough to cover the time it took me to finish my drink, I went back across the yard.

21

Excelling at it

It was only when I fished out the novel I'd been reading in Tenerife that I remembered the two floppy discs. And I only remembered then because one of them tumbled out from being stuck between the pages of the paperback. It already seemed a lifetime ago that I liberated them from the drawer in Los Cristianos. Before ringing Nigel Sutherland and telling him about them, I decided to see if they contained anything worthwhile.

"They seem to be some kind of accounts. Don't know what they relate to, but they're in a spreadsheet. It's an Excel document."

"I wish you'd told me about these last night."

"But I've only just remembered I'd got them..."

The bike courier arrived within the hour, and whisked the discs straight off to Southwark. Sutherland rang me just after it had gone dark.

"You were right, they are accounts. For big deals, too. There are numbers that we have to investigate, but at a guess I'd say they relate to bank accounts. Need to find out where, but that shouldn't prove impossible..."

"Any sign of Lianne?"

"Not yet. The Spanish police are still waiting on their counterparts in Tenerife to trace the villa, and they've not even been able to say if she's still on the island–"

"Something's occurred to me. She could be using her original Polish identity."

"Know what it is?"

"Yes."

Once he'd been given the details, me spelling the surname to him and him reading back to me what he'd written down, he rang off. I put down the phone, and flicked on the kettle to make a drink. Then I stuck a CD into the deck, cranked up the volume, and started thinking about the mess I was in to the strains of Pink Floyd's *Dark Side of the Moon*. By the time it got to the really good bit where Clare Torry wails her way through *The Great Gig in the Sky* I'd worked it all out. There wasn't a damn thing I could do about anything, just carry on going with the flow, keep notes, and pray that enough people would eventually buy the book to numb the pain.

Friday was spent cleaning up the caravan. Although she was staying with Hilda and Alf I knew my mother would at least come in and visit. She did. And Dad too. I cleared all the junk mail and press releases and old newspapers off the table. Washed the bedding, borrowed Hilda's Hoover and vacuumed the carpets, polished all the surfaces. Place looked like new. As a finishing touch I blasted the place with some aftershave. My caravan smelled like a hooker's handbag. I stopped short of nipping to the filling station and buying a bunch of flowers to brighten the place up. The last thing I needed now was my mother thinking I was in the grip of a mid-life crisis.

"This is a nice surprise." I turned to my Mum and asked how she'd managed to persuade Dad to take a weekend off, and to get him away from home.

Before my mother could answer, my father cut in. "We're both going to have to get used me being able to come and go as I please."

"Eh?"

"I've just found a buyer for the business, The deal should be done by the end of next month. So I'm retiring."

"Congratulations!" I was genuinely pleased for him. He looked ten years younger than he had when I was with them at Christmas. I told him so, but as usual, Mum came back with a response before he get any words out.

"And he's booked lessons at the golf club..."

So mine wasn't the only life that had been turned upside down over the past few months. I opened a bottle of white wine that I'd put in the fridge the previous afternoon, and we spent the next hour or so talking about their plans for the future, my imminent week in Melbourne, and the health of the ever-rounder Hilda. All five of us went into Oxford for dinner that night, and my parents headed back for home late on Sunday afternoon. As a parting shot I promised that I would go down the weekend after the business was transferred to its new owners, so that we could go out for a meal to celebrate.

It was probably the first weekend since maybe last July that neither of the Martins entered my head.

That all changed again on Monday morning. Nigel Sutherland rang me even before it was light, to ask me to come down to London. By mid morning I was sitting in the conference room at his offices, with a half dozen other people. The small talk and chink of coffee cups ended abruptly as Mrs Davies tapped her water glass with a pencil and opened the meeting.

"Lianne Martin flew out of Tenerife on Friday, and seems to have disappeared. Those damned Spanish police are useless. She got off a plane in Barcelona, and there's been no sighting of her since. We're still awaiting confirmation, but it seems that the house in the Canaries is in the name of a blind trust–"

I interrupted her, "The one I found out about a while ago that's based in the Isle of Man?"

"Yes. But that traces back via Gibraltar to another trust in Cyprus. The house in Epping is also in the same trust."

"Tidy."

She shot me an insincere smile and carried on. The bank accounts that Nigel has been able to trace from those discs you came across all seem to follow the same route–"

"Meaning?"

"Meaning that she's sitting pretty. The chances of being able to get at any of the money is slim. There is a few million kicking around. Sterling accounts, dollar accounts, Deutschmark, a regular United Nations. And we can't sequestrate any of it. Not even the houses."

"What about her husband's body?" A badly-dressed man with a pencil moustache who I'd seen around, but never been introduced to, used her momentary pause to ask his question.

"He's still in a cold box. The Coroner is going along with the police, and refusing to release the body for a funeral. His sister apparently keeps kicking up a storm every few days, but nobody is playing. We're not gaining anything from it, but it apparently makes the Paddington Green crowd feel happier."

After the bleakness of winter in Oxfordshire it was wonderful to step into the warmth of a late Australian summer. Nev managed to stream us neatly past the usual lengthy immigration queues at the airport, and within an hour of touching down I was slugging back a cold can of Swan on the steps of the Williams motorhome. I looked across at the high wire fence, at the hordes of red-clothed Tifosi streaming along on its far side. Ten of them were carrying a huge Ferrari flag. I took another sip of my beer and decided that this job definitely beats working for a living.

The race went the way of all first rounds of new Formula One seasons, a war of attrition, lots of casualties, disasters for some turning into bonuses for others. The race got under way after a couple of false starts, and within a lap there had already been three retirements. I watched from the trackside as Jarno Trulli punted Damon Hill into the barrier and towards an early bath. I was luckier than Hill was. I used his misfortune as a means of managing to get a couple of shots which paid the rent for another month. And I managed to shoot the sequence of Jacques Villeneuve's race car hurtling towards the concrete wall. He missed contact, but I made it with the pics again. Yet another bonus landed in my lap when Alex Zanardi cannoned off the wall in front of me and my camera. That'd cover the cost of long-term parking at Heathrow.

My hosts were moderately happy with their third place, and the atmosphere over dinner that night was upbeat. I was having a night-cap with Nev back at the hotel when the inevitable question came up; what did I think of all the stuff surrounding Tel Martin?

"There was always something shifty about him. And I'd heard that he's lost the Kentucky money, too–" Nev fixed me with a glance that told me it was down to me to give a verdict.

"Yeah, he has. And as far as I could tell there was no way that he could get anything from anywhere else. All this stuff about bans on cigarette advertising is shrinking the pool of possible sponsors."

Everybody around the table had an opinion. And the overall tone was that Tel had had it coming. Who was I to argue? We were interrupted by Ralfie coming over, ordering a round of drinks so that we could join in his celebrations. Third place in a race where his big brother, the undisputed master of the game, had failed to score a single point was something that the entire team relished. Although he was sticking to orange juice, the euphoria of a victory over Michael Schumacher was enough to have Ralf flying high.

Stepping off a dirty plane a day and a half later, scrambling through the crap on the back seat of my car to find a warm jacket, straightened my head up. I was still a bit groggy from the two diazepam that had helped me sleep. While I waited for the Alfa's V6 to settle into a routine and get warm enough to start the heater working I switched my mobile back on. No messages. Good.

I got home just as the last of the daylight was surrendering, dumped my bag on the end of the unmade bed, and switched on the gas fire. Then went across the yard to blag a coffee from Hilda and ended up staying for a meal. By the time I got back the heater in the caravan had taken five days of chill out of the air. The heat brought the smell of that bloody aftershave I'd used as air freshener back into the atmosphere. I popped another zapper to knock myself out, clambered into bed and slept until

Atilla and his gang of feathered hooligans woke me at dawn.

I heard the phone ring when I was in the shower. If I'd got out I'd probably have been too late anyway, so I ignored it and let the answering machine kick in. Whoever rang didn't bother leaving a message. It rang again as I was finishing off my cornflakes, and this time I answered it.

"Mark. It's me."

Lianne. I was stunned and spluttered out an hello.

"Are you allright? You sound–"

"Yeah, its just that–"

"That I've not been in touch?"

"Something like that... I heard..."

"That I'm out of the country?"

"Um, yes."

"Situations change. But I'd like the chance to explain. Watch for the post in the next couple of days. Bye darlink."

And with that she was gone. What do I do now? First sensible thing is to get dressed. I spent the rest of that day finishing off stuff that I'd started on my laptop in the hotel room and press centre in Melbourne. Restless the next day I went off into the fields with my shotgun. Didn't so much as aim at anything, just walked around for a few hours. Trying to get the mystery of Lianne out of my head, and wondering if I'd done the right thing by not doing anything. One side of my conscience was telling me that I should have called Nigel Sutherland and let him know she'd rang, the other half reasoning that apart from a vague promise of something turning up in the post, there wasn't actually much to say.

I went out for a drink with Paul Laker. Aside of the usual pleasure of being with somebody from a completely different world, I felt that I owed him an explanation. I also wanted to recover the envelope full of photographs and the Zip disk.

"Sorry about the 'dead letter' stuff" I said, as I put his pint of ESB in front of him. "Things were getting a bit hairy for a while and I needed somewhere safe to keep everything that I'd got together on that bloke I asked you to look into last year."

"All sounds a bit sinister."

"Could say that. I got thumped, had burglars, all that was missing was a plague of boils." I then explained as much as I could recall of what had been going on. Three pints later I'd finished the tale, and Paul looked at his watch.

"Jesus, is that the time? I'd better get back. Promised then it wouldn't be an all-afternoon session. Got to finish off a report on some bloody plc."

He stood up, drained the last inch of his beer, and pulled on his coat. "Don't leave it so long next time, eh Mate? And don't go without that lot..." he pointed to the Jiffy bag that was sitting alongside me on the mock-leather seat.

22
Czechmate

The red Escort post van pulled up at about nine on Friday morning. I walked out and met the driver, signed for the brown envelope, and went back indoors. Slitting the sealed edge with a penknife, I emptied its contents onto the table top. Then I rang Sutherland.

"I've heard from Lianne Martin."

"And?"

"And she wants me to go out to meet her. Or at least I presume she does. She's sent me a note. With an airline ticket."

"To? And is it a return ticket?"

I paused to flick through the envelope, checking the number of vouchers.

"You still there, Mark?"

"Yes, sorry, just checking that she wants me to come back. She does. Club Class return ticket to Prague."

"Where? Prague? Why Prague?"

"Yes, seems so. I'm booked to fly out from Heathrow next Wednesday afternoon, and leave there..." I double-checked the return part of the ticket "... Thursday at seven in the evening."

"We'd better get together before you go. Can you come down on Monday? And make sure you've got your mobile with you. I'd like one of our blokes to do something to it."

"Should be able to, Got to go to my parents place over the weekend, but I'll come straight up from there."

I sat dumb-struck in front of the dining table, looking at the cheque. It was Dad who finally broke the silence.

"It's yours. You'll get it eventually anyway and some more besides, but this way you minimise the tax liability. Unless you or your mother bump me off within the next seven years, of course."

Mum flicked her napkin at him, and laughed. "Depends how you behave yourself. And don't get under my feet."

I looked again at the cheque. Four hundred and fifty thousand pounds. Payable to me. I could now afford the Aston Martin DB7 I'd always promised myself. Or a classic Ferrari Dino. Either would transform the drive down from home to Le Mans each year from good to magical. But something deep inside told me that I'd never get either; I couldn't break away from the ethics that my parents had instilled in me. I was too much their son. Don't ask for too much out of life. Don't be ostentatious. Don't be flash. Don't bite off anything you can't chew. God, I blew that last one out of the water when I got sucked into the Tel Martin story... Mum snapped me out of my daydream.

"First time I've known you lost for words since you were about two years old."

"It won't last." Dad smirked, and leaned across to pour me another glass of wine. "It never does."

"Coffee?" Mum didn't even wait for the answer, but stood up and walked towards the kitchen. We could hear her filling the percolator.

"So is this the entire proceeds of the sale?" I was still holding the cheque in one hand as I picked the wine glass up with the other.

"No. Most of it. Most of the cash, anyway. There are some shares, too. But we've kept a bit for ourselves. For a start I've promised your Mum a new car, and we're going to have the holiday of a lifetime, out to San Francisco to see Aunt Celia and then on to an old friend of mine from schooldays. He's a judge in Canberra. Chances are we'll be away for a couple of months."

"When are you going?"

"Haven't booked it yet–"

Mum interjected, bringing through a tray with the coffee cups, cream and sugar. "We've got to wait until your father's finished the handover. They've asked him to be available for a few weeks, to make sure everything's allright..."

"You deserve a really good holiday. It'll make up for all those years when Mum and I went away for a fortnight but you only managed to join us for the weekends. I presume that the new owners are going to leave things pretty well as they are at the mill?"

"So they say."

"Who's bought it, anyway?"

"A Canadian food group who are playing catch-up with some of the other global players. They need a toehold into the British market, and my customer base. They've promised no redundancies, in fact they'll probably be expanding. One of the jobs they want me to do is try and negotiate with the timber yard next door for some of their land–"

We were interrupted by Mum returning, and starting to clear away the dessert bowls.

It had been left that I'd arrive at the Customs offices late Monday morning. As I drove along the M3 heading for London all thoughts of my sudden new riches were gradually displaced. Plans of spending a few days looking around for a house to buy were eased out, to be replaced by thoughts about my imminent trip to Prague. As I tooled up the motorway I wondered what the fuck was going on. Why was she in Czechoslovakia? And why did she want me to go out there?

These questions ricocheted around the inside of my skull for the next couple of days, right until I stepped off the CSA jet. I shuffled through the long queue at the passport desk, answered the same half dozen questions that the uniformed woman had asked the people in front of me, waited while she inspected each page and every stamp that I'd acquired in the six years I'd held that particular passport, then finally got the immigration stamp.

Emerging through the customs exit at Prague airport there was a large bloke ahead of me. He towered over the clusters of reunited families that clogged the concourse. He was dressed in a long black overcoat, and holding a sign in his leather-gloved hand that read 'Mr Mark, Oxford'. I figured it might be meant for me, and it was. Introduced myself, held out my hand.

He took it, shook it, crushed it. Then in halting English explained that "Madam is busy at present, She says that she join you later at hotel." He took my overnight bag from over my shoulder, and led me out to a black Mercedes S500 the size of an aircraft carrier. It had been left right outside the door of the terminal. This guy obviously paid no attention to the usual rules about where you can park. I shivered against the cold, snow still on the ground. Fifteen minutes later we swept through Wenceslas Square (I found this out later, flicking through the free city guide in my room) and I was delivered to the splendour of the Alcron. Again he the ignored parking restriction signs, abandoned the car right outside the front door, and delivered me to the desk. He said something in Czech to the girl behind the desk, then patted me on the shoulder and disappeared. I signed a card, gave her my passport, and was escorted to my room by a porter in his late teens wearing a uniform in its late fifties.

I'd just finished hanging the clothes I'd brought in the wardrobe and stuck my toilet bag in the bathroom when there was a knock at the door. Lianne stood there, smiled, then swept through and kissed me hard on the mouth.

"You look good. It was warm in Australia, yes?" She'd already begun shedding the clean English accent, and reverted to middle-European vowel sounds and diction.

"You look stunning." She did, too. Wrapped in the same mink that had led to an erotic scene in a London hotel last Autumn. I couldn't resist asking her what she was wearing under it.

"A little more, I regret, darlink. This city is so damned cold. But later maybe we can have some fun? Right now, I have booked us a table at a restaurant. The car is waiting. Would you like to change?"

She sat and watched my every move while I undressed, put on my suit, and transformed from traveller into a passable impression of an executive.

"That is a new suit?"

"Yes, figured I needed more than just one, so I went into Oxford yesterday–"

"It looks good. You are lucky, being slim. Most of the men in this city could lose a few kilos. What would you call that colour?"

As I slipped into an equally new pair of penny loafers I explained that it was taupe. I'd been assured that it was the new black, whatever that meant, by the grovelling assistant who'd relieved me of three hundred quid for it...

I put my phone, wallet, cigarettes and lighter into my pockets and we left the room.

She sat almost on top of me in the back of the S500, despite its cream hide-covered seat being bigger than half the sofas in Land of Leather.

"So, are you living in Prague?"

"No, but it's a good place to meet you."

"So where—"

"I'm based in Warsaw, but if you think this place is cold... I'm trying to stay away from there 'til the summer. Then I'll decide what to do from there."

Within five minutes the car pulled up outside a chic-looking place tucked away down a narrow lane, and her driver jumped out and opened the door on Lianne's side of the car. We both got out the same side, and headed for the restaurant door, which was opened in anticipation of our reaching it. The Mercedes' V8 roared into life and it swept off as we entered the little restaurant.

Dark oak-panelled walls, soft lights on the walls, crystal chandeliers, thick dark red carpeting. Rich red tablecloths, glistening crystal glassware and white porcelain tableware that glowed in defiant contrast. They'd probably spent more fitting out this restaurant than had been spent on any of the tower blocks of flats that I'd been driven past on my way from the airport.

Only four of the twenty or so tables were occupied. A maitre d' appeared and air-kissed Lianne on both cheeks twice, then shook my hand warmly. We were shown straight to a table where a bottle of vintage Ruinart sat waiting in a silver ice bucket.

The cork was eased from where it had been since 1990, not with the flourish of a spraying that was familiar in my world of racing celebration, but with a discreet twist and almost inaudible popping sound. The sommelier poured a glass each, then silently withdrew. I raised my glass in response to hers, the tall, slender flutes chinking together tunefully, and we each sipped the champagne. Then she spoke.

"So, you want the rest of the story. Or was it just that you couldn't resist seeing me again?"

I said nothing, just gave her what I hoped was an enigmatic smile.

She started. "I reckon you already know a lot of this, especially as you've been meeting up with the authorities nearly every day for the past few weeks." I felt uncomfortable. She patted the back of my hand. "Don't worry, darlink. Anyway, if that bastard hadn't started screwing around, none of this would have happened–"

She was interrupted by the waiter arriving with a pair of heavy leather-bound menus. Once I'd waded through to find the English language section, studied it and ordered, she carried on. "It was all Terry's idea, you know. Well, it was dropped into his lap, but... But the bastard hadn't got the brains he was born with, just thought he could bully his way through life."

An *amuse bouche* arrived, a little dish each of something with mushrooms. We ate it in silence, then she took up where she'd left off. "It all seemed like easy money. That idiot Paul was easy; he's a gambler, you know, has a bad habit of losing. Kept coming to us for salary advances. So it was easy to get him to abandon his hopes of a percentage."

"And what about the two heavies? The ones who tried to rearrange my face?"

"Yes, sorry about that darlink, they were old friends of Terry's. You know that he use to be a driver, that he'd been involved in a few scams in the seventies, like that Piccadilly bullion thing, don't you?"

"I'd heard the rumours–"

"Well they go back with him that far. But even though Terry was paying their wages they work to their own rules. You shouldn't have been hurt, but they seemed to think you'd gone too far. I only heard that they'd been after you, that you'd been warned off after Terry had been killed... Honestly, Darlink, that was it"

"Did you know they've been arrested? And they arrested Stevenson?"

"Yes, I heard that. I believe he tried to commit suicide, slashed his wrists or something..."

"But how–"

"Just because I'm here and they're all in prison doesn't mean I don't know what's happening. Anyway, I'm paying for their legal representation. Their solicitor is another old friend."

We were interrupted by the sommelier, who topped up our glasses. As soon as he retreated I seized the moment. "But who killed Tel?"

"The Dutch, I think. Those gorilla friends of his thought they were being loyal to him by going out there when the merchandise disappeared. Thought they could sort everything out. But it seems they upset the man in Rotterdam and he thought that Terry had sent them. These greasy biker types don't know what it means to have a calm discussion..."

"I'd wondered–"

"Wondered if it was me? No darlink, I can see why you'd think that way, especially as he'd given that tart the one thing I couldn't have, a child, but no, it wasn't me. I was as shocked as everybody else. Is there any news about the funeral, by the way?"

"Why, are you planning to go?"

"I don't think that would be very wise, somehow."

Another interruption as our starters arrived. As I toyed with wafer thin slices of duck I realised what she'd just told me. "Child? Didn't know about that..."

"Little girl, apparently. She'll be four, maybe five. I had a detective get me some photographs of her... but decided that I couldn't do a damned thing about it. I'd have loved children of my own–"

"So you couldn't–?"

"No. Permanent damage when I was much younger. Before I went to live in England."

"So what are your longer-term plans?"

"I've retired. I retired the day before I drove you to the airport in Tenerife."

"So how did you–"

"I got a call. Like I said, there are people in England looking out for me."

"From what I can gather you and Tel were pretty clever, putting your money into safe places..."

"Yes, darlink. Very safe. I don't really have to work again, ever."

"I'd heard it was six or seven million–"

"I thought you English considered it vulgar to ask about somebody's fortune?"

"Sorry, wasn't prying–"

She laughed, eyes and teeth flashing, and patted the back of my hand again. "You are so easy to wind up! It doesn't make any difference to me. Anyway, seven million is a very low estimate. Whatever, I don't ever need to work again. Though whether I will is something else. I might get bored… I bore so easily."

We spent one last night, screwing hard in the luxury of my suite at the Alcron. She showed me around Prague the next day, and dragged me into a tiny jeweller's shop in a narrow lane in Old Town. Speaking in Czech fluently and comfortably, she bought me a gold signet ring, a gold one with a blue gemstone in one corner and the initial M engraved onto the gold face and L on its reverse. As we left the shop she explained that it would always remind me of her.

"As if I could ever forget" was all I could think of in response.

We carried on walking around the city, then had lunch in the same restaurant we'd eaten in the previous night.

"So where do you go from here? Back to Warsaw?"

She looked at me with a 'don't be stupid' expression. "I'll get by just fine. We'd always planned for being able to live wherever we wanted to. Like I said last night, I'm well provided for."

"So you'll stay out here?"

"Maybe, or maybe not. I haven't decided. I prefer somewhere warmer, Rio appeals. But for the moment–"

"This is what you're stuck with?"

"Yes, something like that." Then she broke into a smile and waved to the sommelier, ordering another bottle of Ruinart.

After lunch we emerged from the restaurant. The S500 was waiting for us right outside, blocking the lane. She directed her driver to take us to the airport. We kissed one last time in the back of the car before I stepped out. My door was opened and I stepped out, being handed my bag by the waiting chauffeur. The door closed behind me.

She lowered the side window. "I'll be in touch. Maybe. Keep your passport handy and don't change your phone number. Not without letting me know. And make sure I get a copy of your book on us! Bye darlink!"

"One last thing." I leaned down towards the open window of her car. "Who was it broke into my place and looked at what I had in my computer?"

"That was Paul, darlink. The first time. The second time was me. G got through the door for me, but I had to see for myself–"

"What second time?"

"Oh, thought you'd have realised..." and with that she pressed the button and the glass slid up. I hadn't gone more than five yards when I heard the driver gun the engine. I turned. She smiled and waved through the back screen and was gone.

I switched off my phone as I settled into my seat on the jet, wondering if it had done what Sutherland's techie had said it would do after he'd finished tinkering with it. Hoping that leaving it under a cushion in the bedroom had been enough to conceal our sexual marathons. And what she meant by the second time.

Aftermath

Nigel Sutherland taps on my window, while I'm shuffling through a stack of music CDs looking for something that I want to listen to on the drive home. "All that stuff that came through on your phone, by the way, it was all good. Pity the Poles aren't going to play the game. Looks like she'll get away with it. She'll probably stay a step ahead of us. God knows she's got enough money to do whatever she feels like."

"Forgot to say. Something that occurred to me when I was flying back from Melbourne. That alias she was using when I went to the Canaries with her. You remember Margaret Thatcher's maiden name was Roberts?"

Free market, free spirit. I look over my shoulder, see that he is still laughing at the irony of Lianne's humour as I drive out of the Coroner's car park.

Stick a disc into the player. Gary Moore's *Still Got The Blues*. He might have, but I haven't; life's never been this good. But his playing's so awesome I stick with it. I've paid off what I owed on the Alfa, had a monster sound system fitted to it, and my new apartment in Burford will be ready next month. I Look at the gold ring that glints between the knuckles of my right hand as the sun catches it. Wonder if there'll be any takers for the film rights to Tel Martin's life story?